All Of You

A Sellwood Novella Book Two

Darla Luke

4 WINGS
PUBLISHING

Copyright © 2015 by Darla Luke
Cover by The Killion Group, Inc
All Of You: Electronic Publication October 2015
ISBN: 978-0-9966699-0-0
All Of You: Print Publication November 2015
ISBN: 978-09966699-1-7

Published by

Publisher's Note: This book is a work of fiction.
The names, characters, places, and incidents are
products of the writer's imagination or have been
used fictionally and are not to be construed as
real. Any resemblance to persons, living or dead,
actual events is entirely coincidental.

All Of You -- 1st ed. by Darla Luke

DEDICATION

Writing is a solitary profession at best, and lonely at its worst. This book is dedicated to my village of friends: the Hooligans & the LOL's...Ginger K, Jessie S, Kim W, Linda K, Linda S, Nancy B, Su L, Wendy W. I can't image a life without you gals in it. This story wouldn't exist without your unfailing support and I thank you from the bottom of my heart!

ONE

Grams wasn't answering her phone.

Mia Belden had called Grams before leaving the Rocking C ranch like she'd promised, but the phone just rang and rang.

Her grandmother probably went to the store, stocking up for Mia's visit. Half-way across the broad side of Oregon, and at every stop for either food or gas, she'd dialed her grandmother's number and left numerous messages on the answering machine.

Grams hadn't called back.

Just outside of the resort town of Bend she'd turned the music off as the insistent murmur of worry turned into a howl with every mile that dragged by.

All the horrible possibilities ran around her brain like a border collie chasing its tail. What if ... damn ... what if Grams had an accident and – heaven forbid – nobody found her?

Or worse.

Her brain froze at the or worse thought. The woman had raised her from an infant. She couldn't imagine life

1

without her opinionated, headstrong grandmother in it.

After hours of driving, Mia battled increasing traffic as she wound her way into the metropolis of Portland, she followed the annoying GPS voice and turned Elle, her aging Bronco, onto the tree-lined street where her grandmother lived.

Eyes burning, she scanned each building, looking for the right set of numbers that signaled she'd arrived. She swallowed the boulder lodged in her throat and refused to cry, putting Gram's favorite saying into action: Pull up your big girl panties and deal with it.

The pounding rain settled into a dreary mist, giving everything a hazy, out of focus quality. When she caught sight of the familiar crooked numbers on the corner three-story apartment, she stopped short in the middle of the road. This was Gram's building?

It looked nothing like the last time she'd visited. Once-clean red brick now had patches of green fuzz, a rusted downspout left streaks like tears and the big front windows were dark and vacant, staring blankly at the street.

What was going on?

During their twice-weekly phone calls, her grandmother hadn't said anything about having financial trouble or that she wasn't able to keep up on the building maintenance. All Gram's talked about was how great her friends were and that she loved living in Sellwood, the small eclectic suburb of Portland.

An impatient driver behind her honked, bringing her back to the present. She focused on the line of cars as far as she could see. Nothing like arriving in the heart of the city during the Friday night bumper-to-bumper, everybody-is-off-work-at-once traffic.

With no parking near the building, she nearly cheered for joy when a car pulled away from the curb a block away. Years of experience paid off as she feathered the gas pedal and urged Elle from a turtle crawl to a hare sprint. When she neared the small section of curb between two mammoth vehicles, a red Mini Cooper spun a U-turn in front of her and tucked into the spot.

Worry for Grams, traffic-clogged streets, and now a parking spot thief all bubbled in her brain, ready to erupt. When a man in a dark blue I'm Important suit climbed out of the clown car, she cracked her window down and leaned out to get his attention. "Hey! That spot was mine!"

Straight out of a manly-man's magazine ad, with spiky blonde hair and round glasses, the hunky guy flashed a toothy grin and gave a full-hand wave before loping to the sidewalk.

Seriously, what self-respecting man drove a Mini Cooper? Her fellow ranch hands would put that toy into the back of their oversized 4x4 pickup truck like it was an accessory.

She raised her fist to give the parking spot thief a one fingered piece of her mind, but envisioning Grams' disapproval stopped her cold. This was her neighborhood, and sure as shootin', she would hear about Mia's lapse in manners.

That was not how she wanted to start her precious few days off.

Elle hissed as steam curled out from under her hood. A quick check of the temperature gauge showed it was peaked into the red, despite the cool, rainy weather.

By the time she found a place to park, the poor Bronco puked antifreeze all over the pavement. Great, just what she needed. The classic truck had been cranky—she was older than Mia—but it had never left her walking.

Finding a mechanic she could trust wasn't going to be easy. And how much was it going to cost? Keeping the old girl running wasn't cheap. Every penny that wasn't earmarked for necessities went into saving for her own ranch. Someday.

Someday never looked farther away.

After locking the door, she patted Elle's road-dirty

red fender and wished she could just turn around and go back to the wide open spaces of Idaho.

The foreman hadn't been pleased when she'd asked for time off so close to the largest sheep fair in the Northwest. He'd agreed to give her an extra two days after the long weekend, then she had to be back on the ranch or her job would be in jeopardy.

Five days. It wasn't enough time to visit Grams for the first time in eighteen months, but it was all she had.

Pulling her overnight bag behind her, she tried the residences' entrance first. No answer after several long minutes of pressing the bell. Clutching the key Grams mailed to her last week—"Just in case," she'd said—Mia went around to store front entrance, the only door with a lock.

Where is Grams? They'd talked on Wednesday, so her grandmother knew she was coming today.

Her impression of the building didn't improve up close. Chipped paint, showing layer after layer of color, framed the store front entrance. Grimy windows prevented her from peering inside. The last time she'd been here, the retail space had been a struggling artist's studio.

A horn honked and someone shouted a greeting, rattling her already frayed nerves. Pedestrians crowded the sidewalk, so she ducked into the entrance with a sigh of relief. She definitely wasn't in the country any more.

The door unlocked with the key Grams sent, but when she caught sight of the interior, she froze, one foot in, one out as her initial dismay turned to horror. Furniture was stacked as far as the eye could see, all piled like a giant Jenga game, leaving nothing but deer trails through the room. A thick layer of dust coated every surface. Cobwebs hung from the bare light bulb like a leftover Halloween decoration.

She should have visited sooner. Much, much sooner.

Grams would never let her house get this dirty. Not

unless there was something very, very wrong. Had her grandmother been sick?

The door closed behind Mia cocooning her in scary-movie silence. A feeling of dread pressed on her shoulders like a heavy wool blanket.

Dragging her overnight bag dragging behind, she made her way through the aisle maze. The room reminded her of a hording show one of the ranch hands watched.

A scraping noise behind a large, ornate cabinet made her jump. Heart pounding, she gasped when a fluffy black cat sauntered from under a nearby desk and wound around her feet with a mournful meow.

"Who are you?" she asked, more to hear her own voice in the dead silence than anything.

A cat. Grams had a cat. And a shop.

With only a small amount of fading daylight filtering through the dirty windows, she navigated the deer trails one hand out and still managed to bounce from one vague shape to another. After what seemed like endless turns and dead ends, a narrow set of stairs yawned in the darkness. She felt along the wall, trying to find a light switch.

A spear of light from upstairs pierced her night-sensitive eyes. "Damn it." She blinked against the brightness, heart thudding against her chest. She hadn't felt a switch yet.

A large shadow clouded the treads, freezing her in place. What the— "Who's there?"

Footsteps thumped down the stairs at a deliberate pace. Her heart sped up until it beat a staccato in her ears. Good Lord, if she had to run for her life, she was so screwed.

Mia dropped the handle to her case and fumbled with her keys for the mace canister bought as protection against Chad-the-Cad, who hadn't taken their breakup well.

"Stop right there, I'm armed."

"Don't shoot," a deep male voice drifted out of the darkness, punctuated by a step-thump closer.

Pepper spray strangled in her fist, she twisted to get a glimpse of the man behind the voice. "Show yourself."

"Contrary much?" His voice was smooth and low with a hint of humor. Long, slack-covered legs appeared in the last bend. Then, a familiar face appeared, complete with spiky blonde hair and wire framed glasses.

It was the guy who'd stolen her parking space.

"What are you doing here?"

"I could ask you the same thing." He frowned and tilted his head. "You were in the Bronco earlier."

"You stole my parking spot. I had to circle the block twice before I could park."

A shoulder shrug telegraphed his lack of concern. "That decrepit vehicle wouldn't fit in the space anyway."

Should she be dialing 911? Her grip tightened on the can of mace. "Who are you, anyway? Why are you in my grandmother's building?"

"I live here."

Wait—what? He might be attractive, with his just-out-of-bed mussed hair, square jaw, and piercing green eyes, but no way Grams would let a stranger live with her. Would she?

"That's not—there's no way—"

He smirked, obviously enjoying himself at her expense. "I have the third floor apartment. Lois has the store here, and the apartment above."

Why would a young, good-looking guy like him live here? Granted, Grams wasn't your typical seventy-something woman, but still...there had to be condos that catered to a younger crowd.

A city guy shouldn't make her heart beat faster, but this one certainly did. Working on a sheep ranch, she was surrounded by men all day, so she'd adopted a "don't date" policy. The ranch hand community was small. Going to work at another ranch didn't guarantee you wouldn't see your ex again.

Yeah, she'd learned that one the hard way.

Out of reflex she checked his ring finger. No band, no tell-tale pale strip of skin of a recently removed band. Stop it. She had neither the time nor the energy for a fling, let alone a relationship.

He saw her glance at his hand and raised an eyebrow in a silent challenge. The white collared shirt was unbuttoned, dark blue suit jacket and tie were gone. He'd rolled up his shirt sleeves, giving him a relaxing-at-home vibe. One she had a difficult time ignoring.

"I'm Nash. You have got to be Mia, the absentee granddaughter Lois talks about all the time." Shoulders rigid and arms crossed, he didn't reach to shake her hand.

Was he mad at her? "Funny, she never mentioned a parking spot thief neighbor to me."

Those movies, where the main character pokes at a sleeping monster to see if it will wake? Yeah, she was starring in this one. He moved closer to stand on the step above her, bringing the sharp, clean scent of soap. Give her dust and a manly odor over cologne any time. She could repeat that refrain all day and would still have trouble believing it.

Nash searched her eyes, peering deep, where most men didn't bother to look. The taunting smile fled. This close, she couldn't help but notice his full, kissable lips.

Heat built between them, pooling in her stomach, then arrowing down to lady parts she'd thought dormant.

He's a stranger.

The reminder was enough to break the spell that kept her immobile. She cleared her throat and stepped back, catching her heel on the forgotten overnight case. Flailing to keep her balance, she was on her way to a broken body part when strong arms surrounded her, bringing her against a hard, warm chest.

"That was close." The words puffed against her cheek. If she turned her head a fraction of an inch, their lips would touch. What would he taste like? Desire darkened his spring green eyes to the color of fresh cut alfalfa hay. Proof of his attraction pulsed against her thigh.

"Wow." She stiffened her back against the urge to lean into his chest as heat crawled up her neck, warming her cheeks. "Um, thanks."

When a mournful meow broke through the tension, Nash relaxed his hold and stepped back. "Trust King George to remind me his dish is empty."

She wasn't sure whether she wanted to curse or hug the cat as she straightened her top and smoothed her fly-away hair back into the ponytail that kept the curly mass corralled.

"So. Uh..." Thank goodness the guys at the ranch couldn't see her now, they'd tease her on how girly she was acting. "The cat's not Grams?"

Nash stuck his thumbs in his front pockets, bringing her attention to the bulge she was determined to ignore. "He came with the building. Don't know if Lois claims him or not. Everyone in the neighborhood feeds and cares for him, but he usually sleeps in the shop or with her."

Dismay must have shown on her face.

"Don't like cats, huh?"

She gulped. Did that make her a bad person? The barn cats at the ranch were around to catch mice. The one she'd tried to make friends with last year shredded her wrist when she'd tried to pet it. "Not really. Moving as much as we did, pets weren't practical. I would have sworn that Grams wasn't a fan, either."

Nash laughed, a nice sound that echoed through the room. "She wasn't at first. George grows on people."

Her unspoken Yeah, right hung in the silence that stretched between them. She shifted from foot to foot, wondering how to get past him. The need to get upstairs and check on Grams grew with every passing minute.

"I should—"

"Do you want to—"

Mia laughed and Nash joined her. "After you," he said, with a courtly half bow.

"It was, um—" She bit her tongue on the first word that came to mind, "—nice to meet you."

"You're staying here, right? Let me show you up to her apartment, the lock can be tricky sometimes."

Where is Grams?

"Thanks, but my grandmother should be home."

"Here, I can take that," Nash said, stepping around to grab her overnight bag at the same time she bent down, almost crashing heads.

She shoulder blocked him with a move she used when sheep were trying to get past her, and snatched the handle of her bag before he could.

"Thanks, but I've been hauling my own bag around for years." It came out sharper than she'd intended. Grams didn't raise a spineless wimp who leaned on others when she could do it herself. Gina, best friend and confidant, often said she was too independent. She was working on it.

"Okay. Be careful of the stairs, the tread is narrow." Nash turned away, a sharp contrast to Chad's sulky tantrums when he didn't get his way.

She was too petite to be Zena, but she wasn't the helpless princess most men assumed. Dating Chad-the-cad was like having a parent telling her what to do and where she could go. When she started to question her own abilities as a sheepherder, she ended their relationship. If only he would understand that.

Nash led the way up the staircase, talking to her over one shoulder. "Lois will be delighted you're here, taking care of her customers."

Customers. This floor was really a store, not just storage? Maybe daylight would improve it, but right now it was so dreary, who would venture in? Then it hit her. A complete stranger knew more about her grandmother than she did.

She barely registered the twists in the staircase as she followed him, all too aware of his tight butt at eye level. At the top was a short hall that lead to a doorway, then turned to another set of stairs which she assumed led up to the third floor and Nash's apartment. Before she could correct his assumption that she was going to be taking care of Grams shop—the shop she hadn't known existed until a few minutes ago—they reached the apartment door. Mia was relieved to see that unlike the floor below, this one was clean and well taken care of.

The apartment was dark and silent. Where was Grams?

As George wound around her feet purring, she struggled with the stubborn lock. "Grams must have sent me the wrong key."

"Here, let me." He held out a broad hand. It took him several minutes of wiggling and jiggling the key in the lock before it unlatched.

The door swung opened on silent hinges, revealing the pleasant space she remembered, with two sets of floor-to-ceiling windows on the far wall, letting in natural light. After seeing the dark, crowded retail space downstairs, Mia had been afraid this floor would be like a dungeon also. Stepping inside and looking around, she got her second—or was it third?—shock of the day.

There were the distinctive lamps Grams bought when they lived in California, and over by the couch were the antique end tables from the house in Nevada.

But…how?

Grams sold everything but the clothes that still fit each time they moved. Or so she thought.

Mia moved across the living room on wooden legs to touch the free-form ashtray she'd made in grade school, sitting alongside a delicate Dresden figurine picked up during their short stay in Washington DC. Everywhere she looked, she found another memento.

Bits of her past she'd thought gone forever.

Only Mr. Squiggles—a stuffed rabbit with spiral, springy ears—survived each move, until he disappeared between leaving Louisiana and arriving in Oregon when she was a teenager.

Nash cleared his throat, bringing her back to the present. "You know, your grandmother is an amazing lady. She took me in when I needed a place to live. So I have to ask...have you come to help her, or be a pain in the ass?"

~ * ~

Nash Anderson clamped his mouth shut. For Lois' sake, he was trying hard to keep an open mind and never intended to say the words out loud. The shock of his words hit Mia like a physical slap, but he refused to take them back. Lois deserved better than an absentee granddaughter who lived an entire state away. Not that the older woman said an unkind word about Mia. Just the opposite. She was always sharing stories of Mia's adventures on the sheep ranch.

With her dark curly hair pulled back in a ponytail, he watched the tips of her ears redden as she strangled the handle of the bag she wouldn't let him carry.

With her shoulders back, there was a fierceness in her eyes as she stared him down. "You don't know anything about my relationship with Grams."

"I know you haven't visited her in the almost two years I've been living here. Where are you when Lois needs help hauling a heavy piece of furniture into that storeroom she calls a shop? Or when she has a fall like she did this morning?"

TWO

Nash crossed his arms as Mia's tanned face drained of color, leaving it ashen. She dropped the handle of her case and looked around frantically. "What? Grams fell? Where is she? Why didn't someone call me?"

It was evident she hadn't known about Lois's accident, but he wasn't about to let her off that easily. "I tried, but couldn't get a hold of you. You might turn your phone on once in a while."

"Cell service is spotty on the ranch." She stalked to the front door and held it open. "Thank you for your unsolicited opinion."

"Do you know which hospital she's in?"

One hip cocked, she crossed her arms, chin up. Defiant. And sexy as hell. "I can find out. How many hospitals are there?"

"Several." He let her digest that for a few moments. "I wanted to see Lois tonight anyway, so I can take you."

Jeez, why was he offering to take her? Something about her intrigued him. The stories Lois told gave him an idea of Mia's strong independent streak, but glimpsing her concern for her grandmother made him want to know more about her.

Then Mia bit her lip, sending arrows of desire shooting to his groin. She was a bundle of contradictions, soft and strong at the same time. He could see she inherited Lois' delicate chin and almond-shaped brown eyes. She was the right height to tuck under his chin and snuggle close. He had to fight the urge to step into her comfort zone to see if she tasted as good as she looked.

What made her tick? Why hadn't she visited Lois in the past year and a half? He knew they kept in contact. The older woman gave him regular updates.

"Fine, I'll follow you in Elle."

Mia's statement interrupted his musings. "Who's Elle?"

She straightened. "My truck." Her glare dared him to make fun of her.

"That beast of a machine that overheated when you parked? At least you didn't name it Brad."

God, he liked riling her, just to see her react. Her foot tapped an impatient beat and warned him he was pushing her near her breaking point.

Good thing Mia wasn't his type. He preferred long-haired blondes, not curly-haired brunettes with a heart-shaped face with an independent streak a mile wide.

The tapping foot sped up as she thought it over. "We might not want to leave at the same time. As you noted, I haven't seen Grams in a while and we have some catching up to do."

When was the last time he'd offered to do a favor for a woman and was turned down? He came up blank. "It's Friday night, so I'm flexible."

She didn't even try to hide the flash of annoyance. "Don't you have a girlfriend, or something?"

He smothered a smile at her probing as he shook his head. "I'm yours for the evening." It was the least he could do for his friend and landlady.

With sharp movements, she stalked to the bathroom

and he heard water running. Was she taking a shower? God, to see water sluicing down her curvy body, slick with soap—

Nash cut off that thought and sat on the couch, trying to think of anything but her naked body. Mia was only gone a few minutes. When she returned, the flyaway hair was slicked back into her ponytail, and her face had a pink glow of freshly washed skin. After grabbing the pink camo messenger bag off the floor, she turned to him. "I'm ready."

Dressed in tight-fitting jeans and a plain tee shirt that hugged every curve, she was radiated a natural sexiness. There were several things he wanted her ready for, and a trip to the hospital to visit his landlady wasn't one of them, damn it.

If he didn't get moving, he was going to do something stupid, like act on his attraction to her. "That didn't take long. No fussing in front of the mirror to fix your makeup for an hour?" Most women slathered some kind of gunk on their face and lips.

She laughed. "I don't do makeup. Sheep don't care if I have gloppy mascara on my eyelashes."

He stopped in front of her and leaned in for a closer look. Wide eyes the color of rich, dark chocolate stared back at him. Cheeks naturally flushed, lips glossy from balm, not a drop of lipstick in sight. Kissable lips, moist from a quick flash of her tongue.

Heat pooled in his loins for the third time that night. What would she taste like? Without thought, he cupped her cheek and angled her mouth for a taste.

Maybe Mia wasn't his type, but she fit against his body like she was made for him.

No hesitation, she angled her head and met him half way. Her lips were soft and tasted like cherry. Never had a lip balm been so inviting. Her hand landed on his chest, and for a moment he thought she would push him away. Then she smoothed his shirt, tracing his pec before reaching up to spear her fingers into his hair.

Knowing she was going to come to her senses soon, he clutched her closer, molding her body to his. Her breasts pressed against his chest, and he longed to strip the clothes separating them and feel her skin to skin.

His hands found their way under her shirt. He skimmed a thumb just under her bra, fighting the urge to strip her bare, lay her on the floor and taste every inch of her skin.

Mia pulled back inch by inch. Her delicate hand caressed his chest one last time before she used it to push away.

"Um, I don't—" She took a deep breath and blew it out.

"Yeah." He nodded and cleared his rough throat. Not the right time, if there was such a thing. Reluctantly, he forced his hands to open and stepped back, giving her space. "So, we should—"

"Sure, let's go."

After locking the apartment door, he corrected her course when she automatically turned to go down the stairs to the shop.

"This way to the street entrance." He pressed his hand against the small of her back, thumb caressing back and forth. Any excuse to touch her again, even if it was platonic on her low back. He had to stop touching her. Soon.

Once on the sidewalk, she stopped short. Her Bronco sat in a puddle of antifreeze. "Oh, man. Can you recommend a good mechanic?"

"There's one close by. I'll give them a call."

"If you give me the number, I can take care of it. Elle's a temperamental beast."

There was that independence again. He was used to taking care of the women in his life.

Before they crossed the side street she stopped on the corner and looked around. "Can't I just catch a cab?"

Afraid to be alone with him, now that they kissed? Her independent streak was beginning to wear thin. "Lois would tear a strip off my hide if I let you take a cab. Besides, you'd have to wait for them, they don't hang around this area looking for a fare."

He guided her to the damned tiny Mini Cooper.

"Not the car I would have pictured you driving," she said as she slid into the passenger seat.

Was she as curious about him as he was her? "What did you see me in?"

"The guys at the ranch all drive pickups, but you strike me as an SUV kind of guy."

He laughed. "When a careless driver ran into my Explorer, the rental agency didn't give me a choice of vehicles."

Mia was quiet during the drive to the hospital, taking notes on a small spiral pad. There were so many questions he wanted to ask, she intrigued him like no other woman he'd met.

Ever since his mom's heart attack when he was in college, hospitals freaked him out. He knew too well the heartbreak and despair when all the medicine in the building couldn't save a loved one. It was one of the many reasons he chose to go into chiropractic practice instead of medicine.

He navigated the brilliant white hallways to Lois' room as quick as possible, not willing to linger in the antiseptic smell any longer than necessary.

They entered the area where her grandmother lay in bed, half-hidden by a privacy curtain. When Mia stopped abruptly, he captured her shoulders to keep from running her over.

She took a deep, shuddering breath. For a few moments, they watched Lois sleeping, surrounded by beeping machines.

Knowing all too well the gut-wrenching feeling when a loved one is lying in a hospital bed, he leaned down and spoke softly in her ear. "You okay?"

At her jerky nod, he hugged her close. "She's going to be fine."

Mia took a shuddering breath and squared her shoulders. Probably preparing herself for the worst. "Thanks."

His friend and landlady didn't look her vibrant self. Lois was as pale as the sheets behind her. Frail and definitely thinner than he remembered from just a couple of days ago.

"Don't talk about me like I'm not here," Lois said, voice sharp. She opened eyes that now reminded him of Mia's.

Mia rushed to her grandmothers' bedside but stopped short. "Grams, how are you? What happened?"

"Better now that you're here," Lois said, reaching a slender hand out to grasp Mia's. "It was a stupid accident."

Mia clasped Lois' frail hand with both of hers and sat gingerly on the edge of the bed near her grandmother's hip.

Not really sure what to do, Nash parked in the corner chair, giving him a view of both women.

Lois smiled and nodded toward him. "I see you've met Nashville?"

Mia's eyes met his, a flash of humor in them for the first time since they met. "Seriously? Nashville?"

He shrugged a shoulder. "What can I say? Mom and Dad honeymooned in the Music City."

Lois shifted with a groan. "Damned hip." With the hand not holding Mia's, she pressed a red-tipped button. "Pain meds on demand. Who would have thought?"

"What can I do?" Mia's gaze darted around the room.

"The nurses are taking good care of me." Lois' eyes took on a sly look he recognized from her many attempts to set him up. "You know, the doctor's a little older than you but quite handsome. Since I'm stuck in this blasted bed, I'll ask him to show you around Portland while you're here."

Mia straightened. "You will do no such thing."

Machines beeped in the background as Nash sat in stunned silence. What. The. Hell? Lois was setting Mia up with some geriatric horn-ball doctor looking for a little fun?

"I'll show her Portland." The words were out of his mouth before he registered what he was saying. He couldn't deny that it felt right.

Identical pair of almond-shaped eyes turned his way. He focused on Mia. From neck to ears, her cherry-red face telegraphed embarrassment.

"I don't need anybody to show me anything." Lips taut, she turned to her grandmother. "I came to visit you."

Given her lack of visits, he thought she'd jump at the chance to see the sights. He thought back to Carolyn, Tori, then there was Nicole, who he almost married, and couldn't say for sure that any of those other women would have turned down a chance to paint the town with an eligible bachelor.

"You haven't had a break since you graduated high school. I want you to enjoy your time here, not be stuck in a hospital with an old woman."

Mia's eyes were shiny. "I want to spend time with you. If you're here, then so be it."

Lois cupped Mia's hands in both of hers. "Promise me you'll let Nashville show you around the city."

"If it will make you feel better." She leaned down to kiss her grandmother's cheek. "I love you."

With a slight smile, Lois' eyes drifted shut and her breathing deepened.

The resemblance between the young and old Belden women was unmistakable. Same narrow chin, same dark almond-shaped eyes. A pixie face and slight build that led a man to think they were delicate, then hit him with their big independence streak.

The privacy curtain rattled like a chain when the

doctor flung it open and stepped in, a nurse on his heels.

"Now, let's see here... um, Mrs. Belden. Broken hip from a fall." He turned to Mia and smiled, all smarmy charm. "And you are?"

"Her granddaughter. Is she going to be okay?"

The doc radiated confidence like a cologne as he stepped close to Mia and patted her shoulder. "Another day or two here, then six weeks of recovery, she should be able to walk again with assistance."

Nash tensed, ready to interfere if the doc got too friendly. If he hadn't been watching Mia's face, he would have missed her shocked look.

"The penguins are coming," Lois mumbled in her sleep.

Doc ignored his patient as he focused on Mia. "For someone of Mrs. Belden's age, a broken hip doesn't heal quickly. She'll be in pain for quite some time. You'll be staying to help her get around when she's released from the rehab center?"

Mia sank down into the chair. "Well, I don't—"

Lois thrashed from side to side. "Don't let 'em take me!"

The nurse rushed to her side, digital thermometer in hand. After a few tense seconds, she read it. "Doctor, her temp is 103.2 degrees."

The doc frowned. "What are her other vitals?" He turned to Mia who watched with frightened eyes. "Is she allergic to any meds?"

"Not that I'm aware of." She twisted her hands together, dark eyes wide and shiny with unshed tears. Nash slid an arm around her shoulders, bringing her close.

THREE

Nash watched the color drain from Mia's face. This was the woman who raised her, how could she not know if her grandmother was allergic to anything?

Lois thrashed in the bed like she fought imaginary demons. "Don't tell Mia!"

Don't tell Mia what? It was clear from Mia's face she didn't know what her grandmother was talking about.

"What's wrong?" Mia shrugged Nash's arm off, chin up as she confronted the doctor.

"She might be reacting badly to the pain medication." Doctor Smarmy dropped his charming façade as he moved away, frowning at Lois's chart. Obviously he didn't have answers.

"Will she be okay?"

"Sure, sure." The doctor scribbled on Lois's chart, then hung it on the end of her bed with a clatter. "I'll write new orders for the nurse. We'll try a different pain killer and I'll be back later tonight to check on Mrs. Belden."

After Doc Smarmy left, the nurse turned to Mia. "I

need to give her an injection, and then change the med pump and lines. It's going to take a while. You're welcome to stay. There's a waiting room down the hall, but visiting hours are almost over. Why don't you go home, get some rest? I'll do everything I can to make her comfortable."

"If she's allergic to the pain medicine, is there anything else that will help reduce her pain?" Mia touched Lois's arm, concern etched in her face.

The nurse shrugged. "It can be difficult to make patients comfortable until we find out what's wrong. We'll call you immediately if her condition changes. Do you have a number we can call?"

"My cell." She dug through her messenger bag, then looked up at him, a pleading in her eyes.

He remembered seeing a pen and note pad on a nearby table and snatched them up. "Here," he said, shoving them into her hands.

She scribbled on the paper and thrust it at the nurse.

"I'll be back tomorrow, Grams." She leaned down and gave Lois a tender kiss on the cheek.

Mia's footsteps dragged all the way back to the parking garage. Such a change from her ground-eating stride on the way in. He wracked his brain for something to say to ease her mind. But platitudes weren't going to make her feel better.

He wanted—no, needed—to do something. "Wanna get something to eat?"

She sagged into the seat, exhaustion etched into her face. "It's been a long day. Can we just go back to the apartment?"

It sounded like something a wife would say.

Warmth settled in his chest as he flashed-forwarded a couple of years, imagining they were leaving the hospital after having their first child.

Nash shook off the fanciful thought. They'd kissed,

nothing more. He glanced at Mia, the streetlights strobing on her heart-shaped face, expressive eyes, breasts he longed to touch. Yeah, he'd like to take it further.

Much, much further.

He had to keep in mind that she was going to leave again. Wild oats and one-night stands were way behind him. If Nichole had accepted his proposal a couple of years ago, he'd probably still be working for someone else. The office he just opened took a lot of his time and energy, making marriage and family years away.

But he couldn't stop thinking about Mia. Was she seeing someone? Some cowboy-type? What did she do all day on the ranch? Lois talked about Mia endlessly, mostly anecdotal stories about the sheep she tended, but he wanted to hear it from her.

"What's it like to run a sheep ranch?"

Mia laughed, a tired sound. "I wouldn't know."

"To hear Lois tell it, you do everything."

Out of the corner of his eye, he caught her rueful smile.

"Grams likes to believe I'm more than just a lowly ranch hand. There's always so much to do, you have to be versatile or you're out the door by the end of your first season."

With her slight build, on the surface it was hard to believe she worked on a ranch. But, he'd felt her defined arm muscles, and the way she blocked him from picking up her bag earlier told him she could take care of herself.

The pieces of her story clicked together. "So, it was a seasonal job, but they kept you on because you're versatile and know more than the typical employee?"

She yawned and sank deeper into the seat. "My bachelor's degree had a lot to do with it."

He stopped for a red light, and watched as Mia's eyes drifted shut and her head slumped sideways. The long drive from Idaho and worrying about her grandmother had taken its toll. He tried to keep the rest of the ride home as smooth as possible, so she wouldn't wake. In the middle of a sharp turn, she slid sideways and landed on his shoulder, a welcome weight. One he could get used to.

Parked in the same spot as earlier, he hesitated. Should he carry her into the apartment? Then her phone trilled. Her eyes flew open as she scrambled to pull the cell phone out of her jeans pocket. He couldn't see the display, but her hunched shoulders and white-knuckled grip said she wasn't happy with whoever was calling.

As the tune faded, she tapped the button to shut it off.

"Not the hospital, I take it?" Nash asked.

Eyes forward, jaw clenched, she spoke through her teeth, "He just can't let go. It's a great reminder of why I broke up with him."

Before he could sigh in relief that she was unattached, Mia was out the door and on the sidewalk.

I don't have time for a relationship. I don't have time for a relationship. I don't-oh, hell.

Anything that took him away from his fledgling practice was a distraction he didn't need, but he wanted to see where this roller-coaster ride would take him.

When he joined her on the sidewalk, twin flags of embarrassment decorating her cheeks. Without a word, he guided her into the building and up to Lois's apartment.

She stopped in the middle of the living room, looking sad and lost. God, how he wanted to gather her close to his chest and make everything better. The possibility that she might haul off and slug him kept his hand in his pockets.

"You hungry?"

She chewed her bottom lip, and he bit back a groan.

Everything she did turned him on. *Focus, Nash. Food.*

"I could eat something." She started for the kitchen.

He grabbed her shoulders and turned her around toward the couch. "Go sit down. I'll make you the Nashville Anderson special."

A quick check in the fridge and pantry told him that he had all the ingredients he needed. Grilled cheese was his go-to quick meal and it was the best he could do with short notice in someone else's kitchen. He silently thanked his mom for insisting he learn to cook at least the basics.

It wasn't long before Mia wandered into the kitchen and hunted through the cabinets until she found a stack of small salad plates. "Think we'll need silverware?"

"Naw, it's just sandwiches." Nash plated the golden squares of cheesy goodness and slid one in front of her. Standing at the counter eating felt right, like they'd been together forever, instead of just a few hours.

He tried not to stare as she took her first bite. "Ummmm," she said, eyes closed, head tilted back. "This is good."

Her face had a look that had his jeans pinching again. How would Lois feel about her neighbor and granddaughter dating? He'd been ready to settle down when he'd asked Nicole to marry him two years ago. Now he was damn glad she'd called it off before they were married, but back then he couldn't see she wasn't the right woman. If he listened to Grayson and a couple of his other friends, he usually dated women who were needy and clingy. Mia was neither of those.

"I'll have to return the favor tomorrow night."

He straightened and smiled. "You'll cook me dinner? It's a date."

She frowned. "Not a date. Return of a favor."

Oh, challenge accepted. "Call it what you want. Say five o'clock?"

She picked up her empty plate and held her hand out for his. "I'll clean up since you cooked."

He lingered in the kitchen while she rinsed the plates and washed the skillet he'd used. Her movements were fluid and graceful and so very feminine. When she yawned a third time, he knew it was time to leave.

"I'll see you tomorrow," he said, willing her to turn and see him to the door.

When she did, her eyes were red-rimmed and shiny. He crossed the kitchen to gather her into his arms. "Hey, Lois will be all right."

She nodded against his chest as she let out a hiccupping sigh. "I know, but she's not young anymore."

"Don't let her hear you say that. She'll skin you alive, and then I'll go hungry tomorrow night."

It got the laugh he wanted, even if it was weak. A quick squeeze and then she pulled out of his arms.

Jeez, he wanted to hold her all night long, if it made her feel better. It would make him feel better. Warning bells rang loud and clear in his head. She was temporary. He wanted permanent, in a few years from now.

"Thank you for everything. I appreciate the ride to the hospital, and dinner." A shy smile snuck out. "And the comforting."

He liked that, for all her strength and independence, Mia wasn't skilled in the man-woman dance. It was all Nash could do to not grab her face and kiss her senseless. Again. All night long.

Her phone trilled again, making them both jump. She silenced it quickly, muttering under her breath, "Persistent bastard."

An awkward silence followed.

"You okay with—"

"Well, I'll see you—"

They stopped talking and laughed at the same time. After another awkward silence, Nash said, "Ladies first."

Mia shrugged and looked down at her feet. "It wasn't important."

"Come on, don't leave me hanging here."

She shifted from foot to foot. "How do you feel about..."

When she hesitated, his mind quickly filled in the blank. *Another kiss followed by some heavy petting?* You bet. *Sex?* He was all for it. *Get married and have two-point-five kids?* Damn, he could practically see a future with her.

FOUR

Bad, bad timing. With effort Nash shut down his rampant speculation and focused on her worried face.

"…Spaghetti?"

Oh, man…she was nervous about dinner tomorrow night? His heart lightened. It was a step in the right direction. "It's one of my favorites."

"Great. See you tomorrow night."

"Works for me."

~ * ~

After Nash left, Mia gathered up the only thing that kept her sane during the long winter months on the ranch…her crochet hobby. Working on the commissioned afghan project kept her hands busy, allowing her mind to wander.

What was she going to do about Grams' situation? The doc said something about six weeks of rehabilitation. Mia couldn't afford to take that much time off, but how could she not?

Grams' accident couldn't have happened at a worse time. Landing a job as a ranch hand at the Rocking C Ranch—one of the sought-after sheep ranches in the northwest—hadn't been easy. Even more difficult when you were female, so she'd worked doubly hard to get hired.

Even though her closest friend, Gina, was the ranch owner's daughter, the annual Sheepherders Roundup was two months away. The ranch was the main event for the first time and Gina's father wanted everything to reflect well on him. It was a lot of pressure on everyone, especially the ranch hands. It meant long days of cleaning up the ranch and getting everything in tip-top shape. Days she was missing.

As her hands flew through the stitches on her hook, the afghan grew in size. She'd hoped to show grandmother what she was working, the older woman taught her how to crochet when she was a young girl.

Then there was Gram's handsome neighbor. Not sure she could trust her instincts when it came to men, she'd sworn off dating and looking for someone to share her life with after the disaster relationship with Chad.

The last thing she needed was another controlling man in her life.

For all his overbearing tendencies to want to do everything for her, Nash genuinely cared for her grandmother.

A mournful meow broke through her wondering thoughts. That cat from downstairs. Should she ignore him? Maybe he'd get bored and go away. She wished she'd thought to get Nash's phone number, so she could call and ask.

Another mournful howl broke the quiet. What to do? She'd seen a couple of small dishes on the floor in the kitchen, so there must be cat food around somewhere. If she didn't let him in, he was liable to keep her, and the neighbor up all night. A vision of Nash showing up in his boxers—or maybe tighty-whities?—flashed through her mind.

Tempting as it was to see what Nash wore to bed,

she couldn't leave the cat out there, neglected. With a resigned sigh, she trudged down the hall to the front door. The black feline noise maker sauntered in like a king. The cat had no shame as he wound himself around her feet, looking up at her like she was the answer to his food prayers.

"Come on. Let's see if Grams left any kibbles for you." Great, now she was talking to a cat.

As she searched the cupboards, she wracked her brain, trying to remember what Nash called him. Maybe a dictator. "Hitler? Napoleon?"

The cat ignored her as he tried to squish his fat bottom into the empty food dish.

Grams was always fascinated with the British royalty. It was something like, "William? Harry?"

Still nothing from the feline doing an impression of a sit-in. "George!"

At the sound of his name, he looked up from his dish. Ah, ha! She grabbed the bag from the bottom of the pantry, then shooed the cat out of the bowl to pour a good portion of kibbles into it. That should keep him for a while.

With the cat taken care of, another jaw-popping yawn overtook her. Most of her evenings on the ranch were spent either talking with her best friend Gina, or crocheting. Her handmade craft order would have to wait, she needed sleep. Ten, maybe fifteen straight hours of sleep sounded good. Her short nap on the drive from the hospital just made her more tired.

She retrieved her suitcase from the living room and headed down the hall. The spare room wasn't difficult to find. When she flipped on the light, another surprise waited on the double bed. Closing her eyes and opening them up again didn't change the view.

Square in the middle of the bed was Mr. Squiggles, the stuffed bunny she thought lost during the last move to Oregon.

But—how? When? Without her grandmother to interrogate, she was left with more questions than answers.

Her eyes burned as she scooped up the only true constant in her young, nomadic life. With Grams in the hospital, Mr. Squiggles could keep her company. She put him in his place of honor at the head of the bed next to the wall.

~ * ~

Mia woke early the next morning and enjoyed a moment of nothing to do. Since graduating high school, she'd been on the fast track to get her degree in search of a stable career. Hugging Mr. Squiggles to her chest, she almost laughed out loud at the idea that her job was stable. Being a ranch hand was fine and everything she'd thought. But stable it was not.

She jumped when someone banged on the walls loud enough to wake the dead. Following the sound to the bathroom, she heard water running. In their brief stay in Washington, she and Grams had lived in an old building where the first rush of water through the pipes made them bang like that. Nash's apartment must be identical to Grams'. That meant, unless he was living with someone, he was taking a shower. Naked. With water sluicing down his hard body.

Heat flushed through her, melting her resolve to stay away from Gram's handsome neighbor. She was only here for another few days, then it was back to the ranch, and her life, such as it was.

George wound around her feet, purring so loud it sounded like a chainsaw. Mia scratched under his chin, thinking about Nash's kindness last night. His calm presence had been a balm for her rattled nerves. His laid-back attitude was in direct contrast to her own type A personality. Unlike the last couple of guys she'd dated,

Nash talked, and listened to her.

After a shower and quick breakfast, she called the hospital and was told Grams was "resting comfortably" and the doctor had restricted visitors until afternoon.

With the day yawning empty before her, the cluttered shop downstairs dinged at her conscience. Even though she was here for a short time, might as well make the most of it.

Descending the narrow, steep stairs, she pictured Grams making this trek several times a day. She'd have to speak with Nash, maybe she could install a motion sensing light. It took several moments groping in the dark shop to find the central light switch, but it only illuminated the dismal state of the room. She wasn't afraid of hard work, but this—this was daunting. Good Lord, hopefully passers-by wouldn't think the shop was open this early. Handling curious customers was beyond her right at the moment.

Before she could tackle the years of dust accumulation, she discovered an office…of sorts. The area had a large, wooden, paper-strewn desk—and the largest shock yet—a computer perched on one corner.

Sinking into the office chair, she stared at the blank monitor screen. Grams had a deep-seated suspicion of all things electronic, but this was proof that she'd moved into the computer age. All those phone conversations, and she never mentioned buying a computer?

"Most of Lois's sales are online."

With a gasp, she looked up to see Nash in the doorway, blonde hair still wet from his shower. She pressed a hand against her thundering heart. "Lord, you scared me."

A smile quirked up the corner of his mouth. "Sorry." He didn't look sorry as he slid into the chair across from her, at ease in the room where her grandmother spent a lot of time, judging by the amount of paper stacked on its surface.

Dressed in casual jeans and an emerald green collared shirt that echoed his eyes, he looked good and smelled like that green soap, sharp and clean.

Nash knew about the computer, the cat, the store and the accident, which was more than she did. What other secrets was Grams keeping?

Speaking with her grandmother twice a week, Mia thought she kept up with Grams life even with hundreds of miles separating them. What other things had she missed?

She swallowed hard against the hurt and turned away to search for the computer's *on* button. She felt Nash's gaze like a caress as she watched the startup screen with a fierce concentration usually reserved for a final exam.

"Anything I can help with?"

She knew when she was in over her head. "So," she cleared her tight throat, "where can I find Gram's online sales?"

Nash sank a little deeper into the chair and crossed one leg over his knee. "When you open the web browser, it should be right there on the start page. You'll need the password."

She searched the desktop for a familiar blue E with a halo. Being connected to the outside world was challenging out in the country, but she thought she was a little more savvy about computer programs. "I don't see one."

With the lean grace of a predator, Nash rose and came around the desk to peer over her shoulder, surrounding her with his sharp, Irish clean scent.

"Here it is," he murmured in her ear like a dirty suggestion. One hand covered hers on the mouse, moving it to the icon that looked like an orange fox face.

She could tell a lot about a man by his hands.

Nash's nails were neatly trimmed nails. Long fingers and a smattering of hair across his strong hands. Hands she could almost feel sliding across her bare skin. A contrast to her own callused hands. She curled her free hand and tucked it out of sight under the desk. Working with sheep, fixing fence and the thousand other things she did in a work day left her hands rough. Soft, womanly hands they were not.

He leaned closer to peer at the screen, his cheek close to hers. "Press here. Yeah, like that."

She shivered as heat arrowed down to her core. Images of them tangled in bed sheets replaced the computer screen. He would be playful, not demanding. Make sure she was satisfied before himself. And possibly, just possibly, give her the first orgasm of her life.

FIVE

Mia squirmed in her seat as heat seared her from the inside out. "Comp—" She cleared her throat. "—Computers aren't really my thing."

"Relax, you'll get the hang of it. Just takes practice." Nash's words puffed against her cheek. If she turned her head, their lips would meet. Again. Good Lord, he kissed like...like she mattered.

He retreated, hands ghosting across her arms, shoulders, back of the neck, somehow touching her intimately with all her clothes on. Or maybe that was her imagination stuck in overdrive.

Sleeping with Nash would be fun, maybe even educational, but she was leaving after getting Grams settled in a rehab facility. A commitment free week of one-night stands was not her style.

But it was tempting. So very, very tempting.

Distraction. She needed a distraction. "So, uh, I was thinking about the furniture stacked in the display area."

Nash's eyes gleamed wickedly and a smile tugged at the corners of his mouth, like he knew her thoughts weren't on furniture, unless it was horizontal and in the bedroom.

Not wanting him to voice what he was thinking, she abandoned the computer. "Maybe we could make it more inviting?" With shaking knees, she stood and rounded the large desk, talking as she went. "It's going to take a lot of cleaning, but I think we can—"

Nash hooked her arm and momentum dropped her into his lap. Their eyes met. Time stopped as she took in the emerald green shot through with golden flecks. Mia licked her parched lips, knowing a kiss was inevitable.

He waited one heartbeat, two heartbeats, three heartbeats. Giving her time to evade, to protest.

Her pulse sped up. She took a shuddering breath. The moment to stop the madness had passed, maybe the instant they met on the stairs yesterday. Not waiting for him to make the first—or was it the second?—move, she ran a hand through his soft blonde hair, learning its springy, silky texture and dove in for a taste.

One hand anchored her hip, the other cupped her chin, angling her head as he devoured her lips.

He tasted of peppermint toothpaste and coffee and long nights and slow hands.

Clever fingers brushed along her side, under her top. Skin that hadn't felt a man's touch in a long time. Certainly never this tender, this reverent. He took his time, learning what made her squirm, what made her freeze, not wanting to him to stop the delicious torture.

Hands that had a slight roughness, surprising her. She'd expected soft, pampered city-boy soft-as-a-baby texture that would put her off. For the first time, she wasn't disappointed to find out she was wrong.

Not to be out done, she tugged at his shirt, exposing the chest she'd only felt through fabric. Silk over steel, hard and soft at the same time. Springy hair the color of sun-bleached grass dusted the vee between his pecs, a narrow trail disappearing beneath his waistband. She traced that trail downward, eager to discover where it led.

He broke the kiss, breathing hard as he stopped her questing fingers just above the point of no return. "Are you sure about this?" Green eyes pleaded with her to be positive this was what she wanted.

She bit her lip. Her heart pounded in her ears. Loud and rattling.

"I think—" Lord, she wanted to continue her exploration, as much as she wanted anything right at that moment. But, was she *sure* it was the right thing to do? "I think there's someone hammering on the shop door."

Nash exhaled his disappointment and kissed her hard before loosening his grip so she could clamber off his lap on unsteady legs.

She straightened her clothes and smoothed her wild, curly hair with shaking hands. Her nipples were diamond-hard with wanting. His hands. His lips. If only she could convince her body that sex with Nash was a monumentally bad idea.

Glad to cool down and put a little distance from him, she made her way through the deer trails of stacked furniture to see who want in the shop this early on a Saturday. As she neared the dingy glass, she saw two indistinct shadows, with the smaller dog-shaped shadow at their feet.

Her steps faltered. Her face felt hot, lips swollen. Could she be nice to people in her current mood?

Nash's hand landed on her shoulder as she unlocked the door and stepped into the opening. His body heat bathed her back as he crowded close.

"Good morning, Nashville." The other woman's gaze bounced from her to Nash. She looked to be a little older than herself, maybe mid-thirties. Dressed in similar short-sleeved shirts and khaki shorts, the couple could almost pass for twins, except the man had caramel colored hair and held the leash of a beautiful golden-haired dog.

"Morning, Sam." He nodded the man's direction, then the tall woman's. "Sydney. What has you two out this early?"

Sam and Sydney's gazes bounced from her to Nash behind her, then to each other. Sam hid a grin behind a fake cough. Good Lord, was it that conspicuous that they'd been making out? Mia straightened her top and touched her swollen lips. She wanted to slam the door and punch something, preferably Nash, since he was hovering close.

The golden retriever crowded in with tail-wagging delight and no judgment. Mia knelt down to get a slobbery kiss, grateful for the distraction and the distance from Nash.

"We stopped to see Lois. Is she okay?"

When Mia hesitated giving out information to strangers, Nash leaned down and spoke into her ear, eliciting a shiver. "The Adam's are friends of your grandmother. And that's Goldy, their golden retriever."

Mia smiled, her face tight with worry. "Grams had an accident. She fell and broke her hip."

The other woman gasped, free hand pressed against her stomach. "Oh my gosh, that's terrible. Is there anything we can do to help?"

"No, but thanks. When I called this morning, she was resting comfortably," Nash said.

Her heart melted. He'd called the hospital this morning like she had. A warm glow bubbled in her chest, threatening to close her throat. All her growing up years, it had just been her and Grams.

She couldn't hide behind the dog forever, so she gave him a good scratch behind his ear, then stood and faced the couple shoulders back, daring them to say anything.

"We live in the neighborhood and visit Lois every

Saturday. You must be Mia, she talks about you all the time."

Remembering the long-winded descriptions of the people in Grams' life, Mia eyed the two standing in front of her. Could this be the couple her grandmother told her about? She'd pictured them older, closer to Grams age. "It's nice to meet you."

"How is life on the Idaho farm?" Sam asked.

Mia smiled, liking the couple more and more. "It's a ranch."

"Same thing, right?" Sam said, with a crooked smile that probably charmed the pants off his wife.

She started to correct the man—politely, of course—when Sydney put a hand on her husband's arm.

"Honey, a farm grows food. A ranch raises livestock. Or horses." She looked at Mia to back her up.

Mia's shoulders tightened, remembering how much work there would be when she returned. "It's a sheep ranch."

They looked at her like she just spoke Russian. Cattle and horses, most people were familiar with and understood their use. You could eat one, ride the other. What did a person *do* with sheep?

"Lois said you were in charge of the entire operation," Sam said brightly, like he was trying to make up for his misconception.

Mia laughed, picturing Roger's face if he heard that one. "I'm a lowly ranch hand."

Someday, she'd manage a breeding operation, or better yet, own a small ranch of her own. Every dime that wasn't earmarked for living expenses went into that someday dream.

She could almost hear Grams voice, scolding her for keeping her friends standing on the stoop in the hair curling mist. "Would you like to come in? I'm not sure where we can sit down..."

Sydney shook her head before Mia finished her sentence. "Thanks, but we've got to be going."

"I'll let Grams know you stopped by and asked about her."

"Well, it was good meeting you, Mia. Nash. Tell Lois hello for us, and that we hope she recovers soon," Sydney said.

Goldy cold-nosed Mia's hand and she leaned down for one more scratch behind the dog's ears. "It was nice meeting you."

"We hope Lois gets up and around soon." Sydney paused. "We'll bring a casserole or something. Do either of you have food allergies?"

Mia shook her head, and caught Nash doing the same out of the corner of her eye.

"Great." Sydney glanced at her husband. "I think we have the makings for enchiladas."

Sam slung an arm over his wife's shoulder and gave a jaunty wave. "Let us know if we can be of any help."

They turned to leave, and then Sam stopped. "Lois mentioned a new shipment coming in," Sam said, nodding toward the shop hours painted in gold on the door. "Will you be keeping the shop open?"

"We'll have to see." Mia cringed inside. Dealing with customers was a lot different than dealing with sheep. Sheep were simplistic animals. Food, water, lambs and making lambs. "I might need someone to run the shop. If you hear of anybody who would qualify, let me know."

Mia closed and locked the door. The silence left behind was broken only by the cars driving by and pedestrians hurrying down the sidewalk past the shop.

Now what? Would they pick up where they were interrupted? She glanced at him, trying to gauge his mood. Would he be a gentleman and not mention their near sexcapade in the office?

"So, what do you want to do now?" Nash grinned, showing off dimples she wanted to taste.

When it came to elective hard, physical labor, most guys she knew disappeared or made excuses to leave. Time to see what Nash was made of. Hands on hips, she sized him up and down. "How would you like to be my slave for the day?"

Four hours later they were both sweating and dirty. As they worked, Nash never missed an opportunity to trail his fingers over her hip, caress her butt or brush her hair from her face. More touching, in or out of bed, than all her previous boyfriends combined. Her nerves hummed with want.

When her stomach rumbled for the third time, reminding her she hadn't eaten in hours, she held up her hands in a T formation. "Time to take a break, I'm starving."

Nash stopped in front of her, settling hands on her shoulders. "Me too." The gleam in his eyes told her it wasn't food he was hungry for.

He pulled her close, inch by inch, giving her time to protest. The dust streaks on his face, the sweat-stained shirt, it all disappeared as his lips settled on hers. This kiss was different than the first two. This was exploration and patience. It was long-term and I'll-be-here all rolled into one. And it was scary as hell.

As his tongue danced with hers, hinting as to what would come, she heard a bell trill. Nash ended the kiss slowly and pulled back to gaze into her eyes.

"I think we have a customer."

Not the words she expected. Her head finally cleared enough to hear two women talking in the next aisle.

Nash gave her a hard peck on her lips, imprinting his desire. "I'll take care of the customers, then we'll talk about why this guy keeps bugging you."

Sure enough, the familiar tune she'd attached to Chad-the-Cad played merrily from her messenger bag.

Couldn't Chad take a hint? She pulled the phone out and hit the phone icon to answer it. "You have to stop calling," she said in lieu of a greeting.

"Hey, babe. I miss you. When you coming home?" His rough tone once thrilled her, but it seemed she preferred a city man with a deep, silky voice and hot kisses.

She turned and walked into the office, not wanting the customer, or Nash, to overhear. "We broke up. Why can't you get that through your thick skull?"

"Aw, why you gotta be that way?" His words slurred. He'd been drinking again. "I love *you*."

Last year she might have waffled, believing he was sorry and wanted her back. Time and distance gave her the prospective she'd needed to know, deep down, that he was never going to change.

"Stop calling me. We. Are. Through." She ended the call, not certain he would remember their conversation, or the ten before that.

Walking back into the front display area, she put Chad into the dark recesses of her mind reserved for regret as she marveled at the work she and Nash had accomplished in a few, long hours. Sunlight spilled into the room through clean windows, highlighting the furniture that gleamed from hours of dusting and polish. A sparkling crystal chandelier hung above the expensive Louis XVI dining set. It smelled like lemon and oil, a huge improvement over the musty, dark area they'd started with that morning.

A tall brunette and her brown-haired friend exclaimed over an antique bedroom set like it was a pile of designer shoes. "It would go perfectly in the Western room." The older brunette placed a hand on Nash's arm with a flirty smile. "We'll take it."

Mia could see the furniture wasn't the only thing she'd like to take home.

While Nash finalized the sale, she ignored the jealous pang and hunted down wherever Grams stashed the linens, her steps more like stomping. So they'd kissed a couple of times. And indulged in a heavy petting session. It wasn't like they were involved in a relationship or anything. He was a free man, he could take the woman up on her not-so-subtle offer.

When she returned with a box of doilies and tablecloths, the flirty woman and Nash were nowhere to be seen. In no time she had the linens decorating the dining area so it looked like it would in a home.

Visions of the woman and Nash making out fueled her determination to get Grams settled tomorrow and return to the ranch where she belonged. Was there any faithful men left in the world? She seemed to find the ones who thought monogamy was an outdated concept.

Half-an-hour later the front door bell chimed when Nash returned. He had brown paper bags clutched in one arm and drinks in another. Her relief in seeing him warred with the visions of him and the customer earlier.

"Hope you like Pad Thai."

Great. Her mouth watered. Breakfast had been hours ago. And Thai food was scarce in Podunk, Idaho.

He headed toward the office, so she dashed around the desk to clear a spot, her movements sharp with remembered anger. Mia could feel his gaze on the top of her head but she refused to meet his eyes.

"Are you upset about something?" he asked as he piled cardboard takeout containers in the cleared area.

"Nope."

Out of the corner of her eyes she saw him stop, shoulders slumped as he rubbed the bridge of his nose. "I thought you were mature, and past the 'I'm angry but don't want to talk about it like an adult' type of high school drama."

Good Lord, he thought she was acting like a teeny-bopper?

SIX

Nash took it as a good sign when Mia sank into the desk chair in slack-jawed shock. He expected her to pull away, or close up like a turtle. It was clear from her reaction to his caresses all day that she wasn't used to much outward affection. As she worked out her shock, he divvied up the food. They ate in silence for a while.

"My last boyfriend was a control freak, then cheated on me."

She let that conversational bomb sit there for a few dozen heartbeats.

"The guy who keeps calling?"

She flinched. "Yeah."

He had to force food past the lump in his throat. "How long ago was the breakup?"

"Eight months, when I caught him humping a buckle bunny. In his truck." She sipped her soda. "But when he drinks, which is often on the weekends, he calls and wants me back."

"Next time he calls, let me answer." He smiled at her wide-eyed surprise. "Nothing discourages a guy more then another in his place." Or it could backfire, but that was unlikely as long as Mia was sure the relationship was over.

She stared down at her plate. "When you were flirting with that customer, it—uh—hit me wrong."

Ah, the crux of the matter. It was a good sign she was jealous, but not if she was going to use it to push him away. "Tell me what you saw."

"She flirted with you."

He nodded.

"Why didn't you discourage her? Unless you wanted to—"

"I'm a guy. Unless I'm dead, I'll always want to." He reached out and entwined his fingers with hers. "But, when I'm with someone, I'm in, one hundred percent. As long as I can enjoy the view, I don't have to sample the wares."

A grin snuck out as she ducked her head. "No one has been that frank."

He felt his smile fade as he stared into her eyes. "I will. And I want you to be honest and open with me. No judging, no pressure."

Mia pulled back, shaking her head. "I'm not staying. I have a job to get back to."

He tugged on their entwined hands. "One day at a time. Think you can do that?"

When she nodded, joy threatened to send him soaring. It was like he'd just caught the winning touchdown in the civil war football game or aced his chiropractic exam on the first try. He wanted to give her anything she asked, as long as she just kept looking at him with those sparkling, chocolate brown eyes. "Okay, now that we've established that"—her fingers tensed in his—"let's go visit your grandmother."

His unexpected answer made her laugh. "Not what I expected you to say."

It didn't take a mind reader to know that she thought he'd jump her bones right then. Not that he didn't want to, his pinching jeans could attest to that, but he wanted their first time to be special, not just a quickie hoping a customer wouldn't walk in.

Like the night before, they cleaned up the lunch debris as if they'd had years of practice.

"How did you and Grams meet?"

"I'd just opened an office next door to her shop. She struck up a conversation and I was looking for a place to rent. I'd just lost Nana, and she filled that gap. Made me feel less lonely."

"That sounds like Grams. What kind of office is it?"

"I'm a chiropractor."

She straightened from wiping the table and looked him up and down. "Yeah, I can see that, you have great hands. Do you specialize in anything?"

He smothered a smile at her perceptiveness. "Prevention as well as recovery after an accident. My patient load is growing and I have ideas to expand and offer new services."

"Just after starting at the Rocking C Ranch, my wrist started hurting and going numb. I thought it was carpal tunnel until my friend Gina convinced me to go to a chiropractor. After one adjustment, it stopped hurting."

"Bones out of alignment cause a lot more pain than you would think." He grabbed a broom he's used earlier and swept up around the table.

"What do you usually do on the weekends, when you're not a slave to distressed sheep herders?"

He stilled. Normally he'd give a glib answer that he chased after little old ladies or something. The words died before they left his mouth. If they were going to have a chance at—something—he had to be frank and honest with her, as he wanted her to be with him.

"Cleaning out Nana's house. She's been gone a couple of years now, and it's time." He nodded toward a stack of furniture they hadn't had time to deal with.

"Some of this was hers and Papa's."

She moved close and put a hand on his arm. "I'm sorry."

Memories assaulted him. The long hot days, laughter from various visiting cousins, swimming in the nearby creek. "I used to spend summers on the farm, helping with the harvest."

Her smile was tinged with sadness. "Sounds wonderful. What did they raise?"

"Lavender, gladiolus. Vegetables, raspberries. She had a roadside stand that Papa built from scrap lumber. People would come from miles around to buy eggs from her hens."

"Sounds like a great childhood," she said, echoing his thoughts.

"The best. There was always work to be done, but Papa let us have fun." He took a deep breath to ward off the heaviness in his chest. "The farm has been in our family for over three generations."

"Wow, a Century Farm. What are you going to do with it?"

"Sell it, I guess." He shrugged like the idea of selling wasn't tearing his childhood to pieces, which was probably why it was taking so long to get the property ready.

Her shoulders fell. "Such a shame. Nobody wants to run the farm?"

"We all have careers, and farming on a small scale doesn't pay."

Nash shook off the wish that he could somehow keep the place and his chiropractic clinic in Sellwood. He dismissed the fantasy. Farms needed full-time care.

"Are you ready to go?"

She ran a hand through her hair and looked down at her dusty clothes. "Give me a few minutes to clean up, okay?"

By the time he'd locked the front entry and turned off lights, Mia was back, kissable lips glossed, hair tamed, and she'd changed into a clean top that didn't have his dusty hand prints on it, damn it. He liked marking her as his.

God, how he wanted to muss up her hair and tumble her down on the floor for more heavy petting that would lead to a happy ending for both of them.

Instead, he guided her out the back door and to his rental car.

After he slid into the driver's seat, Mia turned to him. "I'd love to see the farm while I'm here, if you have the time."

Of course she'd be interested, he should have offered. "Sure," he said, trying to figure out what would be a good day to go. It wasn't that far outside of town, but with his work and her taking care of her grandmother, it might be tough. "Maybe next weekend?"

She turned away to stare out the windshield. "Sure, if I'm in town."

Once the car was moving, he asked the question that had been bugging him for a while. "You know, Lois has never mentioned...what happened to your mother?"

Mia's laugh was sad. "I can't imagine losing a child, even a grown one, is ever easy to talk about. Just after I was born, Mom went out to get diapers, and a surprise snow storm swept through. A semi slid into her car. Grams said she never felt a thing."

Even though she was too young to remember, it must hurt a little to tell the story. He reached over and grabbed her hand, thumbing her knuckles in silent sympathy. It was telling that she didn't pull her hand away until they reached the hospital parking garage.

When they walked into Lois' hospital room, a distinguished older man he didn't recognize stood close to the bed, one hand gripping Lois'. She giggled like a school girl and a healthy flush tinged her cheeks.

Mia stopped short and he had to grab her shoulders so he wouldn't run her over.

"Looks like you're feeling better," Nash said to break the tension thick in the room.

Mia sent a questioning glance at the white-haired gentleman beaming at them.

"Much better. John, this is my granddaughter I was telling you about." Lois turned to give Mia a frown that clearly said "Mind your manners."

"Mia, this is John Barrett. His wife Martha and I were friends when we were younger. I lived next door to them when I was a young bride."

Nash felt Mia's shoulders tense under his hands. The flowers on the bedside table and Grams flustered actions hinted that he was more than a friend.

"Nice to meet you," Mia said, her voice soft and questioning.

"Likewise." John reached over and shook her hand, his face open, body relaxed like he had nothing to hide.

Nash stepped forward into Lois' view. "Nashville Anderson, but call me Nash."

"It's nice to meet ya'll, but I have to get back to the house before Zack—he's my grandson and runs Martha's Elder House—sends out a search team for me." The older man leaned down and kissed Lois' cheek, causing her eye lashes to flutter.

There was a long, heavy silence after John left, broken only by the sounds of machines beeping in the background.

"He seems nice," Mia said finally, her voice neutral.

Was this the first time Lois had a gentleman friend in her life? It explained why Mia didn't know how to react.

Lois' mouth firmed in a straight line. "What, you think I don't know nice people?"

Mia crossed her arms. "Sam and Sydney stopped by this morning. They're worried about you."

The older woman's eyes narrowed at Mia. "They look out for me. Like Nashville."

Ouch. The accusation hung in the air like a bad odor.

After a sideways glance at him that showed her hurt and sorrow, Mia sank down on the bed. "I'm sorry I couldn't come to see you before now. First the blizzard in the mountains right before Christmas, then lambing season started early—"

The doctor chose that moment to waltz in the room, clipboard clutched in one hand, pen in the other. "Mrs. Belden, how are we doing today?"

Lois shot the doc a mutinous look. "I don't know how you're doing, but I'm fine."

Oblivious, Doctor Smarmy plowed on. "We need to keep you another day or two."

Mia straightened, one hand on Lois' shoulder. "Why?"

"We'd like to run more tests."

"For a broken hip?"

The doctor ignored Mia's question. "How have you been feeling lately, Mrs. Belden? Before the accident?"

Lois plucked at a loose thread on her covers, a mutinous frown between her brows. "A little tired. Get out of breath easily."

"You didn't mention it the last time we talked," Mia said. The look in her eyes hurt to see. More secrets that Lois kept from her granddaughter.

"I'm old. It's to be expected."

"What do you think is wrong?" Nash didn't like where this was going, so he moved closer to Mia.

The doctor didn't bother to look his direction. "Congestive heart failure."

~ * ~

Mia rubbed her brow where a headache tightened like a band.

Congestive heart failure. "So what does that mean?" She clutched her hands together to stop the shaking.

Nash moved to stand close to her shoulder, giving off an *I'm here for you* vibe. The problem was, could she trust a near-stranger?

"Fluid has built up around her heart, making it work harder. Now it's tired. We'll prescribe medicine to help the heart work. She'll have to cut out table salt and watch her daily intake of salty foods. Eat healthy. Take potassium. Check her ankles and feet for swelling. Most people with this condition, if they watch their food intake, can live another five to ten years."

Five to ten years? *It's possible Grams could live for only five more years?*

It wasn't long enough. In the back of her mind, she had a long time to save money, get established and buy a farm. Then she would build Grams a small house and they would live close so Mia could take care of her.

"We'll keep Mrs. Belden until Wednesday, then discharge her to a rehab facility. The head nurse will talk over the options with you."

The words bounced off Mia's brain like they were speaking Chinese.

Finally the nurse and doctor left and they were alone in the room, the blood pressure machine beeping quietly in the background.

"Why didn't you tell me you weren't feeling well?" Mia asked, gripping Grams' thin hand.

"I didn't want to worry you. I thought—" Grams sighed and picked at a loose thread at the edge of the thin blanket. "I thought it was old age creeping up on me."

Fatigue etched deep lines in her grandmother's face,

something Mia hadn't seen in a few years. Usually right before they sold everything—or so she thought—packed a few personal possessions and moved again.

"I'm sorry I wasn't here." Mia took a deep breath and let it out slowly. "But you should have told me."

"What could you have done?"

"I don't know. Something." It was crazy busy at the ranch, and always a feeling that someone wanted your job. But she could have done something. Then she remembered all the list of things she wanted to talk to Grams about. "What about all the other stuff you've been keeping from me? You have a store, cat...any other secrets?"

Vaguely she heard Nash say something about getting coffee and leave the room, giving them privacy.

"Nothing that you need to know about." Grams shifted, then grimaced in pain.

Mia's mind raced with all the things her grandmother could be keeping from her. Did she have siblings she didn't know about? Was she adopted? She thought they had a close relationship, it hurt to know that her elder matriarch kept things from her.

"You mentioned something in your sleep yesterday. What secret don't you want to tell me?"

"I don't know what you're talking about."

It was Mia's turn to sigh. It was going to take more than Grams' mulish denial to derail her.

"I'm not a child. Whatever you've been keeping from me, I can handle."

Grams stared out the gap of the privacy curtain as she played with the loose thread again, eyes unfocused.

"I know you don't have a lot of reasons to trust him, but Nashville is a good man," Grams said, eerily close to Mia's thoughts earlier. "If anything happens to me—"

Because of their gypsy lifestyle, there hadn't been a lot of constants in her life, but her grandmother had always been there for her. Mia swallowed past the golf ball-sized lump in her throat and tightened her grip on Grams' hand briefly. "You took me in as an infant and raised me as a single parent. You're the strongest woman I know. Nothing is going to happen to you."

Grams sat up straighter, fierce brown eyes drilling into hers. "I want you to promise, if anything happens to me, you'll let Nashville help you."

"Okay, I promise," Mia said, voice strangled.

When her grandmother settled back onto the pillows, Mia relaxed, not realizing how tense she had become.

"It wasn't easy on you, moving so often when you were growing up."

The change in subject startled Mia. Looking back on her life as an adult, she saw how Grams had done the best she could. As a child, when she would lie in bed and long to settle down, she blamed her grandmother's gypsy lifestyle.

"It couldn't have been easy for you, either. Saddled with a baby after you lost Mom." The reminiscing was so not Grams. She wasn't one to dwell on the past. Really, what was the point? You couldn't change it.

"After your mother died, your father took you to live with him."

SEVEN

Mia sat in stunned silence for several heartbeats, not sure she heard correctly. "Wait—what?"

"You were too little to remember, but you lived with your father for six months after Melynda died."

Fear sent shockwaves through her body, immobilizing her for a moment. Mia put a hand on Gram's bony shoulder. "You don't have to—"

"Seth was ... he was troubled—"

So that's what "troubled" meant: drunk and threatening.

"—and didn't know how to take care of you. He loved your mother very much, and losing her was like losing his rudder through life."

Cold chills ran down her arms. All those years of dreaming of a perfect father who would blast into her life and give her a perfect life crumbled to dust. She barely registered when Nash quietly slipped into the room and slid a hand over her shoulders, hugging her close, offering warmth she so desperately needed.

"It was a long battle, but the judge awarded me custody when you were three. Seth wouldn't give up. Said you were the last thing he had of Melynda."

Why was she learning of this now? Her mouth opened and closed, but no words escaped. Years of wondering. Years of questioning if her dad wanted her, loved her.

"So we moved. And Seth found us, harassed me, threatened to take you and disappear."

Mia had vague memories of her father pounding on the door in the middle of the night, yelling. "That's why we didn't stay in one place for more than a couple years?"

Grams nodded, eyes sad.

It was because of her, moving often, never settling in one place. Never putting down roots.

All the years angry at her grandmother, blaming her for the constant moving from another city to another town to another state, never having roots, a place to settle. To find out that wasn't true was mind-boggling.

"Why are you telling me all this now?" Grams could have kept it to herself and Mia would have never known.

"Seth showed up at the shop last week. He wants to see you."

No, no, no. She shook her head as a vice squeezed her chest, freezing the air in her lungs. That man would not come back into their life and threaten it. She was not moving again, and neither was Grams.

Nash leaned close, anchoring her with hands on her shoulders. "Breathe, Mia."

She took a deep breath automatically. "Why?" She broke away from Nash's embrace and paced the small scrap of floor. "Why would he show up now?"

"Well, he—"

"Wait—did he push you? Is that how you fell?"

Grams shook her head, reaching up to stop her frantic movements. "I'm a clumsy old woman. George wound around my feet, and I missed the last step."

Without the cat's timely interference, her grandmother's heart condition could have developed for years before it killed her. But without Seth's appearance, would Grams had been so distracted?

Her stomach rolled, threatened to bring up the Pad Thai from lunch.

"Hand me my pocket book." Grams waved a thin hand toward the wall. "It's in the closet." Mia retrieved the purse then helped her into a sitting position.

Her grandmother dug into the cavernous purse and found her wallet. She held out a small stack of bills with a white slip of paper. "You probably haven't eaten. Here's money for food and his phone number. Call him."

Mia shook her head and refused to accept either. "We ate before we came here." Bits of her childhood nightmare filtered in. Her dad would show up at their current house, banging on the front door, back door, windows. Always yelling her name. Always drunk.

She held up her hand like a traffic cop. "I don't want to see him."

Her friends had fathers or step-fathers that would take them to the park, or a movie, showed them how to ride a bike. They were in the audience of the Christmas play or spring recital. She wanted a dad like that. Not a belligerent drunk they had to hide from.

"It's your choice. But take the phone number."

Mia stuffed the money back into Grams purse, but crumpled the paper and stuffed it into her pocket, out of sight. Her grandmother sank back onto the pillow, eyes droopy and tired. "He's changed, honey. At least give him a chance."

"We should go, let you rest. I'll see you tomorrow." Mia leaned down and kissed a papery thin cheek. "I love you."

It was all happening at once. Grams accident, her heart condition, now Seth wanted to see her. The urge to jump into Elle and drive until she couldn't drive anymore was almost too much to ignore. Except, her truck was still broken and she had to wait until Tuesday to get it fixed.

All through the hospital Nash walked by her side, guiding her around obstacles she didn't see, silently offering support.

"Why is Grams Seth's crusader all of a sudden? She should have kicked him out on his butt, or better yet, call the cops and have him arrested." Mia all but stomped out to the car in the parking garage, mind whirling with all the implications of her father wanting to see her. "Why now?"

"You won't find out until you meet with him." Nash started the car, but she couldn't concentrate on where they were going.

Her neat little world was crumbling. What was she going to do?

Nash covered her wringing hands with his. "If you don't want to go alone, I can come along and make sure he keeps civil."

She shook her head. "I'm an adult. He can't grab me and run. And why would he?" What she remembered of her father was a larger-than-life man. Skyscraper tall. Scary big, with a barrel chest.

He squeezed her hand. "You're not alone. Let me help."

Her heart did a quick two-step at the thought. These past couple of days he'd been a rock. But she'd been wrong before.

~ * ~

The week passed by in a blur of touring short-term rehab facilities that would help Grams recuperate, navigating the confusing world of financial responsibility, and a myriad of other decisions Mia couldn't recall if her life depended on it. She called the mechanic to look at Elle, see if she could be fixed, and called Roger, the ranch foreman, to extend her leave.

Nash was easy to be around. Gina would say he was easy on the senses. He didn't force his opinion, or try to change her mind. On the drive back from visiting Grams one evening, she didn't recognize the route.

She sat up straighter. "Where are we going?"

Nash smiled, making his eyes crinkle and light within. Her heart did that weird two-step again. "Keeping a promise to Lois. We're going to a Portland tradition. I've been told every out-of-town visitor must go here."

He parked in an open curb spot. It happened several times in the hospital parking garage and now here. "You're a parking spot savant, aren't you?"

"Naw, just good at spotting them." He opened the door for her and guided her up the sidewalk. This part of town was quirky, but had an almost industrial feel to it. Then they would pass by open-air shop, with incense so strong it made your eyes water. At least, she thought it was incense.

He looped an arm across her shoulders, keeping her snug against his side. It had stopped raining, and the air had that fresh, clean scent.

Colorful yarn in a store window caught her eye. Nash stayed with her as her steps slowed. "What do you see?"

"Heaven." Without thought she left Nash behind on the sidewalk. The door opened with a tinkle of a bell. No incense here, just an explosion of color as far as she could see. Hanks and skeins of all colors rested in shelves, lounged on table tops, slouched against mannequins who pretended to knit.

"May I help you?"

Mia turned to the tall woman with a smile. "Do you have any soft, bulky-weight yarn?"

"Certainly." The other woman turned and headed to the back wall. "Do you knit or crochet?" she asked over one shoulder as she walked.

"Crochet. I make afghans to sell."

"Any particular color you prefer?"

"Emerald green." Mia sighed. "I haven't been able to find anything, but then again, there aren't a lot of yarn or craft stores in the closest town."

The clerk led her right to the color she'd been looking for. Unable to help herself, she picked it up and ran her fingers through it, testing the softness and bulk. Even with her callused fingers, the strands slid across like silk.

"It's baby alpaca yarn," the clerk said. "Has a great hand feel, doesn't it? The color dye is not water-soluble, so it can be washed. It's recommend to air dry it though."

"It's perfect." Mia checked the yardage and did some quick math. "I'll take eight skeins." Her hands itched to get started, now that she had the perfect color.

After paying for the yarn, she found Nash on a bench near the front door, obviously put there for that purpose judging by stacks of gun and car magazines spread across the coffee table.

"Find what you needed?" He stood and looped an arm over her shoulder.

She nodded as he tucked her close. Nash guided her toward a long line of people. *No, no no.* They weren't headed for that line, were they?

She breathed a sigh of relief when he turned into the alley. "What's that line for?" Mia asked, looking back over her shoulder.

"Voodoo Donuts."

She'd heard of it. Funky names, weird combinations of flavors like a bacon maple bar. The smell of frying sweets hung in the air, making her mouth water. But a bunch of fried dough wasn't worth standing in a line that disappeared around down the block.

"I thought you wouldn't want to wait in a long line, so I called in a favor."

The smell of cooking pastries got stronger as they neared an unmarked gated door. Nash knocked three times, and a frosting-splattered woman answered holding a brown paper sack.

"Hey, Nashville. It's been a long time."

Nash's face reddened and he shuffled from one foot to another. "How have you been, Nicole?"

Nicole was a dark blonde, with lighter blonde streaks in her hair to resemble time spent in the sun. Looked like she got her tan from a booth, not any actual outdoor activity.

Mia wanted to hate her.

"Good." Nicole held out the bag, and when he closed the gap to take it, she moved in with both hands on his chest and leaned in to plant a lips-to-cheek kiss. "I just can't thank you enough for recommending me to the owners. You're a doll."

Who was this woman? The green-eyed monster chewed away at her brain and she clamped her lips closed against the things she wanted to say. Nash backed up out of the woman's reach, paper bag clutched on one fist.

"Nothing to thank me for. You had the qualifications and got the job on your own merit. I just put two and two together."

With his free hand, he brought Mia close enough to tuck under his arm. "This is Mia. Mia, this is my former girlfriend."

"It's good to meet you," Nicole said to her, then looked at Nash. "You're doing okay?"

"Doing great. The clinic is open."

"I'm glad for you." Nicole smiled and turned to her.

"Nash is a good guy, just not the one for me, know what I mean?"

No. How could he not be the one for her? Mia nodded anyway, since it was expected.

"Thanks for the donuts, Nicole." Nash sounded far away as exhaustion settled into Mia's bones.

Neither said a words for a few blocks, the silence heavy with everything unsaid between them.

"You're friends with your ex?"

"This is the first time I've seen her in almost two years. After I proposed and she turned me down, we didn't talk for a long time."

Mia stopped walking and faced him. "You don't owe me an explanation."

He took her arms and pulled her close, staring into her eyes. "Yes, I do. You're important to me, and I don't want you to think that Nicole has any place in my life anymore. She burned that bridge a long time ago."

You're important to me. For as long as she could remember, it had been her and Grams against the world. Nobody had ever said she was important to them. Important enough to take time out of his busy life to see her sick grandmother. Important enough to see someone who had broken his heart.

They walked another block before Nash spoke again. "What are our plans now that Lois is settled?"

"Sydney gave me the number of someone who might be interested in watching the shop during the week."

If the woman worked out, it was one item off her long list of things to accomplish before she had to go back to work.

"Is it your plan to herd sheep for someone else for the rest of your life?"

She shook her head. "I want to own my own ranch. Have sheep, maybe even card my own wool and make yarn."

He nodded. "I have tomorrow off. The auto body shop called and my truck is ready. After I turn in the rental and pick up the truck, maybe we could visit the farm before we see your grandmother?"

Something in her unwound at the thought of wide-open spaces and less noise bombarding her all the time.

EIGHT

Nash's offer was spur-of-the-moment, but when Mia's shoulders unbunched and her expressive brown eyes lit from within, he knew it was the right thing to do.

"That sounds great."

At the entrance to the Chinese Gardens he steered her in, then paid the admittance fee. "Here's the other part of the evening."

Mia stepped inside, looking everywhere at once. "This…this is heaven."

He breathed a sigh of relief. She'd looked tense and ready to flee the city. Mia looked everywhere at once, taking in the peace and quiet. He kept glancing her way and knew the moment she started thinking about her father and his unexpected return in her life. Her eyes got that wide, frightened-deer-in-the-headlights look.

"Hey, it'll be all right. For right now, let's enjoy the gardens." He took her hand and tucked it into the crook of his arm. "Mom brought me as a kid. When I've had tough decisions to make, or just need to recharge, I come here."

"I needed this. Thank you."

They strolled the paths until they came to a bench partially hidden behind foliage. "So where do you see yourself in five years?"

She flinched. "Well, I thought I'd be running a farm by now. Maybe not my own, but at least be a foreman for one of the smaller sheep operations. Opportunities are not as available as I'd thought. What about you?"

He smiled. "I'm in the middle of my five-year plan. Opening the office and getting my practice off the ground were the first steps."

She asked more questions and appeared interested in his plans for the future. They walked for a while, enjoying the serenity of being surrounded by plants.

They ate donuts, talked and laughed until the gardens closed.

Being with her was a natural as breathing. She didn't fill the entire time with questions, and offered suggestions that he couldn't wait to implement.

She had a quirky sense of humor that made him belly laugh more than once. The park closed at dark, so he guided her toward the car.

At the Mini Cooper, he pulled her into his arms, like he'd been aching to do all evening. Unlike the first couple of kisses, this one was all about learning her, what she liked, what made her breath hitch.

He cupped her face, brushing his thumbs across her cheek. She tilted her head and kissed back, meeting him tongue to tongue.

Her hands tugged at his shirt until she could slip under his shirt, brushing her fingertips over his sides, back, chest. His hands were busy learning every curve and angle. Exploring every inch of skin until he thought he would make love to her right there. It wasn't until a young voice yelled "Get a room!" that they broke apart, breathing heavily.

"Let's go back to Grams'," Mia said.

On the drive, she keep a hand on his knee and he almost missed a couple of stop lights. He was so hard it was painful. Mia was everything he needed in a woman. He'd always been drawn to the women that were clingy and helpless, and he'd been the hero. With Mia, he could relax and have a partner in life, rather than a dependent.

He still wanted to take care of her, that wouldn't change, but she could take care of herself. A helpmate, partner in life, rather than a child in a woman's body.

There was always the possibility she'd change her mind on the drive, but her hand on his thigh, stoking the fire, pinky sliding down into the crease where his thigh met the groin, told him that possibility was slim.

He thanked his lucky stars traffic was light, his attention was focused on all the things he wanted to do with her, to her. The drive felt like an eternity, and it was over too soon. Mia grew bolder and brushed a pinky over the part of him that wanted attention desperately. Another time, he'd let her explore and he'd endure the sweet, sweet torture. If they didn't slow down, let the fire boiling inside him settle down to a simmer, this was going to be all over before it started.

Car parked and shut off, he gathered her into his arms for another kiss. He cupped her face, brushing his thumbs over her cheeks, wanting to touch every inch of her body, head to toe and back up again, lingering here and there.

Her hands snuck under his shirt, sliding over his sides, chest, then lower, and lower. He sucked in, giving her fingers the space to dip below his waistband. He followed her lead and explored her soft skin, brushing over her breasts, teasing her nipples.

They were breathing hard when they broke apart. Seeing his window of opportunity, he grabbed the keys, bolted out of the car and around to her side to open the door.

She was giggling as she took his hand like a princess, and rose gracefully out of the car. Thanking his stars for remote locks, he barely registered the acknowledging beep as they sprinted for the building.

Mia's laugh was infectious. Heart lighter than it had been in years, Nash laughed along with her, loving the silliness of rushing into the stairwell like mischievous teenagers.

Once inside, he tugged her into his arms, pinning her against the wall. He needed to feel her, skin to skin.

Tugging on her top, she helped by raising her arms above her head. Top gone, he kept her hands in the air, giving him access to her bra-covered breasts. Kissing down the arch of her neck to her nipples, he loved one, then the other through the material, making her moan.

She gathered his shirt and tugged it over his head. Done with the barrier between them, he unclipped her bra and it released her breasts into his hands. Kissing her, he gathered her close to feel her soft skin against his chest. *Heaven.*

Mia reached between them and he sucked in when she found the button on his jeans and with a twist, it was open. She lingered on the zipper, teasing him until he was weak in the knees with wanting to be inside her.

Not to be left behind, he tugged her jeans down to her ankles and it was a race to who would be naked first.

Mia won by reaching into his briefs and freeing him. Hard enough to cut glass, he thought he would lose it before he pleasured her. He pulled her panties down over her hips, reaching the spot guaranteed to make her forget her own name.

"Wait, what about—"

"Yeah," he said, releasing her for a moment to grab his pants and dug in the pocket for protection before quickly rolled it on.

He rubbed and teased that magic spot until she said

"Now!"

With a thrust, he seated himself to the hilt and stopped. It felt so good, he just wanted to linger. But Mia had other ideas. She lifted her leg up over his hip, seating him even deeper. When she reached down to touch him, he had to count backward from one hundred to make it last for her. Hands full of her breasts, he teased her nipples to fine points, then went back to the slick nub that would send her over the edge.

Fast, slow, he rubbed until she was panting. He was close, but she had to go first. When she grabbed his butt to pull him closer, he sent her over the edge and followed.

They stayed fused together while she trembled with aftershocks. Several moments later, she sighed. "Wow."

Heart full, he chuckled, touching his forehead to hers. "That good, huh?"

"Yeah. First. One. Ever."

The breath froze in his lungs. Did she just say…"First time?"

She started to pull back, cheeks a pretty shade of red. "What's the big deal? So I never—"

"It is a big deal." He didn't let her get away, still loving the feel of being inside her. "You've never had an orgasm before? Selfish bastards."

"Well, more like selfish bastard."

He was her second lover? Almost worst then being her first. But, when he thought about it, it didn't surprise him. She lacked a practiced hand at seduction that charmed the shit out of him. Guilt attacked him. "We should have made it to the bed, at least."

Mia laughed, short and sweet. "We weren't exactly patient."

He pulled out, still hard, and zipped up. He wanted her. Again. And again.

She looked around, and he gathered up her top and

bra while she pulled up her pants. It was such a shame to cover up her perfect breasts, so he sprinted up the stairs. "See you in the apartment."

"Wait-my top! My bra!"

He turned and waved them in the air from several steps up to show her he held them hostage. "Come and get 'em."

~ * ~

Mia froze, shocked, then realized how fun it would be to catch him. Giggling like a school-girl, she chased him up the stairs, holding her boobs so they wouldn't flop around like water balloons. He was quicker than she thought. At the apartment door, she almost tripped over George, who meowed pitifully and wound around her feet. She stopped to scratch the cat's head and watched Nash disappear down the hall to the bedroom.

She longed to follow. But the cat needed fed, and she needed to catch her breath, at least emotionally. Confessing her virgin status with orgasms was difficult. Making love to Nash wasn't a mistake…falling in love with him would be.

She wasn't here to stay. Grams would recover and she'd be back on the ranch in Idaho. Her time here was just a magical interlude. She shivered with the thought, a chill down her spine that had little to do with being topless. Before she could come up with excuses to call their lovemaking on the stairs a one-time deal, Nash snuck up behind her and cupped her breasts, enveloping her with his heat. Massaging, tweaking. It felt so good, so right.

Later. She'd end things with him later. She leaned back, letting doubts and worries fade away.

His hand trailed down to her sex, still sensitive from their earlier lovemaking. With a few well-placed fingers, the pressure built. Higher. Higher. Heart full, she let go as he sent her into orbit again.

Her knees turned to water, but he held her against him while she trembled with aftershocks.

Nash kissed her ear, neck, shoulder. Never letting go, he scooped her up and carried her down the hall to the bedroom like a bride.

Lovemaking the second time was no less intense than the first. She tried to focus on his pleasure, but he knew all the right buttons to push to launch her into orgasm again, and as she shuddered with satisfaction, he swiftly followed.

He took care of the protection and came back to bed, pulling her close. Skin to skin. Eyelids heavy, she drifted in a warm cocoon of contentedness. In the past, she was restless after sex, feeling empty. This cuddling afterward, heart-full-to-bursting sensation was new.

She drifted off to dreamland before she could figure out what that meant.

The next morning, Mia woke to a heavy arm pinning her down. She untangled herself from Nash and threw on his shirt against the chill of the apartment.

So many things bounced around in her head, it was difficult to pin down any one thing to think about. Her foreman from the ranch had left a voice message the day before, asking when she expected to return. How she missed the call, she'd never know.

Seth's phone number throbbed like an ache in her mind. Nash's advice was to see him, Grams wanted her to give him another chance.

He was her father, the only one she'd ever known. That he'd been lousy at it shouldn't be a factor. What was it like to love somebody so completely your life was wrecked when you lost them? She shivered, afraid of the answer that popped immediately to mind.

Scrap of paper crumpled in her hand, she dressed as quietly as possible and went downstairs to jog off some of the tension and decide what to do about her father.

The neighborhood was Sunday morning quiet as she started out slow, taking her time to really look around the area. Quaint shops, a tea house located inside a train box car, a mismatched sock store—omg, how could she have missed that? She had to admit, the area was growing on her. It had a small-town feel to it, an insular community.

By the time she'd run the tension out of her muscles, she knew what she had to do. Outside of interviewing in the male-dominated field as a sheepherder, the phone call was probably the hardest thing she'd ever done.

The western-themed coffee shop she'd seen on her run wasn't busy, thank goodness, but it was still a public place. When Seth walked in the door, six-foot-one with a barrel chest and a head of thinning curly red hair, all she wanted to do was jump up and run like her life depended on it.

As he got closer, she could see the damage a hard life in the bottom of a bottle had done to his face. Instead of the smooth skin she remembered, he had lines creasing his cheeks and the broken blood vessels across his nose looked like a road map.

"Mia," he said, his voice deep and gravelly…and straight out of her nightmares. "Thanks for calling."

She steeled against the fear that flashed through her, igniting every nerve. "Grams said you'd changed, turned over a new leaf." If she left now, she'd never know if it was true.

Eyes downcast, he fidgeted with a napkin. "You want coffee? I can—"

She stood. "That's okay, I'll get it. I just wanted to see if you'd actually show. You want anything?"

He flinched at her not-subtle barb. "Sure. Black."

Ordering and bringing the cups back didn't take long, and did nothing to settle her nerves. That part of her who longed for a father in her life wanted to jump for joy and babble like a little girl, tell him about Nash and all the things crashing around in her head.

Mia had vague memories of the times when he'd appear in their life, yelling and threatening to take her. Then they'd pack up and move. Again. And again. Not something she could get over in an instant because he said he'd changed.

She set the paper cup in front of him and settled in the chair, stomach pitching and rolling. Seth took a drink, then pinned her in the seat with those blue, blue eyes. Sorrow pulled at the corners of his eyes, shiny with unshed tears.

"I'm sorry. For all the things you went through." He sighed and clutched the coffee cup with white-knuckled hands. "Crap, that's not what I meant to say. I'm sorry for all the things *I* put you through."

Not the way she pictured this conversation going. She wanted to scream out all the sorrow and rage and hurt she bottled up all those years. She wanted to tell him what she went through. Moving, changing schools. Losing friends. Never having roots.

But the deep sadness radiating from him said he'd lost a lot himself. If this was what happened when you loved someone, so much that your world crumbled when they were gone, she wanted no part of it. Her heart clutched and beat unevenly as she pictured Nash, hair mussed from her fingers running through it.

She wanted to be mean. Hurt Seth like he hurt her. But it wouldn't make her feel better.

"Where are you staying?" Dang, what if he was homeless? What would she do, take him back to Grams' apartment?

His face brightened when he grinned, showing uneven teeth. "I have a small apartment in Portland. Well, Gresham really. Got a job at a carpenter shop, building cabinets. The owner's real nice, taught me the trade." He fiddled with his cup, turning it round and round.

He was nervous. That realization eased her own anxiety.

"How about you? What do you do?"

She told him about her college years, and being a shepherdess on a big ranch. As she talked about her work, she realized that she missed her friend Gina, but didn't miss working at the ranch as much as she missed working outdoors with the animals.

By the time they'd finished their second cups, the shop was bursting with customers. She'd left Nash a note, but missed his smile and infectious energy. She had a lot to tell him. Plus she needed to visit Grams. They had a lot to talk about.

"This was nice," she said, standing and gathering her stuff.

Seth—she couldn't think of him as her dad yet—held out his hand. "I'll take care of our trash."

Mia handed her paper cup over and watched as he wound through the coffee-deprived mass of people to the garbage can, heart thumping with gratitude. He seemed to genuinely want to get to know her.

They met back up outside the door. Should she give him a hug? He was a stranger to her still, but he was her father. He took the choice out of her hands when he gathered her into his arms.

He smelled like coffee and Old Spice cologne. She didn't have memories of her mother, and the ones she had of Seth had been shrouded in fear and fog. She hugged him close, glad she took a chance to meet with him.

"When do you go back to Idaho? Can we get together again?"

Mia stepped back, heart bursting with hope that she

could get to know her father and replace the fear with acceptance. "Yeah, I'd like that. I'm here through next weekend. Hopefully Grams will be well enough so I can go back to work."

Even as she said it, a part of her wanted to just say to hell with it and stay in Sellwood. She waved goodbye and started back toward Grams' apartment, a spring in her step. She couldn't wait to see Nash, tell him about her visit.

~ * ~

Nash woke to the persistent feeling of being watched. He cracked open one eye to see George sitting on the empty spot next to his head. That he was alone didn't surprise him. Mia was used to her solitary life style and it would take time to get used to having someone beside her.

He stretched, not wanting to get out of bed, but wanting her again. Hell, he just wanted to see Mia, be with her ... see how she was doing after last night. Dang, that was new.

In the kitchen, George wound around his feet, purring loudly. The cat dish was half-full of food, and he had water, so Mia must have fed him. But where was she?

He let the cat out, gravitated toward the coffee pot, and found a note on the counter. *Went for a run. Be back soon. Mia.*

After a quick shower, he heated up a pan to start breakfast. A few minutes later he heard the downstairs door. Mia strode in, hair pulled back in a ponytail, top molded to her breasts, face flushed from cold air and exercise.

Nash stopped, struck by the thought that hers was the face he wanted to wake up to every day for the rest of his life.

"Good morning." He set the spatula on the counter

and gathered her into his arms despite her protest that she was sweaty. "Did you enjoy your run?"

She smiled, eyes sparkling. "Very much. I, uh—"

He kissed her. All he wanted was to pick her up and carry her to the bedroom like he did last night. But then they'd spend the day in bed, and he had plans.

They broke apart. "I'm making food. It's just about ready."

She looked dazed, eyes unfocused. Good, maybe he had a chance to change her mind about going back to Idaho. "I need to shower."

"Sure, breakfast will take a little bit."

"You're always feeding me. Dang, I just realized that I've never cooked you dinner." She got the plates and silverware out to set the table.

"I'll take a rain check," he said, wiggling his eyebrows.

Her laugh at his suggestive comment filled a hollow spot in his heart. If only she could see that they were great together.

Just as he was plating the hash browns and eggs, she came into the kitchen looking like his dream woman. Her curly hair dark still wet, tee shirt molded to those breasts he couldn't get enough of, and jeans riding low on her hips. Dang, she made his whole body shudder with delight, just by walking in the room.

"So, I just—"

"Do you want to—"

They both stopped talking and chuckled. After a game of 'you first' Nash gave in. "Do you want to go with me while I take care of the rental and pickup? Then we could go from there to visit the farm. I should spend some time out there, do a little work. Then we could stop by to see Lois on the way home."

Her face lit up and she bounced on her toes like she couldn't contain her excitement. "That's a great idea."

NINE

At the farm, Mia looked around and breathed a deep, filling her lungs with the smell of gladiolus and lavender blooming. The house was large and had lots of character. At one time it was white, but now was more of a dingy gray. Weeds had grown up in the yard and field, giving it an abandoned look that tugged at her heart. She could see it as it once was, a thriving farm with kids running around and families coming from all over to buy healthy, organic food grown right there. Maybe even picking their own.

Nash led her up the back steps and unlocked the rear door to the house. "It was built by my great-great-grandfather for his bride. He brought her here from Nebraska with her prized set of wedding china on her lap the entire journey."

The décor was straight out of the seventies. Avocado green and harvest gold. But the wainscoting in the living room and high ceilings gave the space a warm, inviting feeling. Some of the rooms were small, others just right. It wasn't a showroom house, but one meant to be lived in.

The kitchen stole her heart. Bright light, the sink centered in front of a bay window that gave a great view of the side yard and fields beyond, as well as a couple of storage sheds. She could even see the farm stand out by the road. Everything needed a fresh coat of paint, maybe some boards replaced. The raspberry and blackberry bushes held several pieces of antique farm equipment hostage.

Tall trees stood sentry over the lane from the road, and green fields as far as she could see.

"What do you think?"

She turned to him, sure her heart was going to bust out of her chest. "It needs work, but it's beautiful."

"I have to clear some limbs that fell in the last storm, and mow the lawn. You can sit on the back porch if you want."

"Do I look like a princess to you? I can help."

It took them several hours of back breaking work, but they finally had all the limbs picked up and ready to be cut up for fire wood. Mia washed her hands in the kitchen sink and looked out the window as Nash walked by with the last load of branches in his arms. His face brightened to a big grin when he caught her looking. The picture he made, muscles bunched, sweat dripping, made her heart stutter.

In that moment, she saw a future with Nash. A blonde little boy with his eyes, following daddy's every step, a dark-haired girl with his grin kneeling beside her, pulling out flowers as well as weeds. Or vice versa, she didn't care.

Her body stilled. No, no, no. This was fantasy, not her future. Marriage and family were not for her, it hurt too much when you lost them. She was not going to make the same mistake Seth had.

Maybe she could buy the farm? Dang, she didn't have enough for a down payment yet. It might take her another year to save up enough.

Nash came in a little while later. "You know, I was thinking…after we visit Lois, you could call your father and see if he has time to meet us after dinner."

She turned and leaned back against the counter, hugging herself. "I forgot to tell you, I met with Seth this morning."

The hurt on Nash's face made her heart clench. "I thought you went out for a run? Why didn't you wait so we could go together? It could have been dangerous for you."

"While I was out running, I had time to think. We met at a public place, I'm not stupid."

Nash paced across the kitchen floor and back. "I wanted to be there for you. Present a united front, so he couldn't hurt you anymore."

He saw them as a couple, even though he knew she had a life and a job back in Idaho. Dread pressed down on her shoulders, making it hard to breathe.

The ringing from her messenger bag gave her the distraction she so desperately needed. When she pulled out her cell phone, she saw Gina's number on the screen. Trust her best friend to call when she was panicking. She went out the back door so she could talk freely.

"Good timing, Gin. I was—"

"You have got to get back to the ranch right away." Gina's whisper made her forget all about her own crisis.

"What's going on?"

"Dad's in a snit that you're not back to work and the Sheepherders Festival is next week. He asked me to put out feelers for hiring another hand to take your place."

"But, Roger okayed my leave until next week. What changed?"

Gina's sigh came through the phone loud and clear. "It might be my fault. I called off the wedding."

"What? Are you crazy? Your dad hand-picked

Roger for you. Ranch foreman marries ranchers'
daughter. It's almost a Hallmark made-for-television
movie."

"Yeah, well...maybe that's the problem. Roger is in
love with the ranch, not me."

Mia thought the same thing. Roger hadn't acted like
a man in love, but what did she know?

She took stock. Grams was in a rehab facility, but
Mia hadn't called the number Sydney gave her for the
woman who might be interested in watching the store.
She'd have to call on the way.

"Okay, I'll drive back tonight. See you then." After
hanging up the phone she didn't move for several long
minutes. She felt Nash's presence behind her like a force,
but couldn't face him for several long moments. The
ranch was her life, not here. It was nice to get away and
live a fantasy for a while, but it was past time to get back
to the real world.

"You're leaving?" Nash asked, his voice carefully
neutral.

Mia nodded, still not looking his direction. It hurt
too much. Better to rip the bandage off all at once. "I
have to get back to the Rocking C, now that Grams is
settled." She dropped the phone she'd been strangling
into her bag.

He didn't say anything, just stood there.

What about us? He didn't have to say it out loud.
The question rang in her ears like a church bell.

"Can I trouble you to take me back to the
apartment? I have a long drive ahead of me."

"I'll lock up the house." His voice was flat, dead.
Like a polite stranger who hadn't kissed her senseless or
made love to her on the stairs.

She waited in his truck, arms hugging herself,
stomach clenching. In a matter of minutes, her dreams
crumbled to the ground like a sand castle in a storm.

Nash's cold silence during the drive back to Gram's apartment spoke volumes.

Once parked, she didn't wait for him to open her door, but bolted as soon as he shut the truck off. She stumbled on the stairs where she had her first orgasm and nearly face planted. Every reminder of what she was leaving behind cut a little deeper. She had to leave. She had to leave.

She had to leave.

"What about Lois. You're just going to leave without saying a word?"

What about us?

"I'll call her from the road. She'll understand."

Mia randomly threw clothes into her suitcase until she had everything but Squiggles. The bunny sat on the dresser, reminding her of lonely nights as a teenager. Reminding her of lonely nights to come. She avoided looking Nash's direction as she stripped the bed they'd made love in.

She turned to leave, hoping for a quick exit, but froze when she saw George sitting in the doorway watching her frantic movements. "Will you feed him?"

Nash stood in the middle of the room, arms by his side, fists clenched. "Of course." She saw him swallow hard. "Want me to take your bag downstairs?"

To reject his help now would doom their relationship for ever. Something she couldn't do without ripping out her heart and stomping on it.

"That would be nice. Thank you."

He nodded and picked up the overnight bag like it was a feather. Once they reached the sidewalk and the bag was stowed in the Bronco, there was an awkward silence. Jeez, tackling a wayward sheep was much easier than navigating the minefield of a relationship.

"I guess I'd better get on the road."

When she started toward Elle, Nash stopped her

with a hand on her arm. With just that light touch, her resolve to leave wavered.

He turned her to face him, cupped her cheeks and kissed her hard. Imprinted. Branded.

"You will be back." He said it with certainty.

She swallowed hard and nodded. "Sure. Next weekend."

Mia left Nash standing in on the sidewalk as she unlocked Elle. Her faithful Bronco was right where she'd parked a week ago, after the mechanic fixed her. A thin film of dust on her windshield the only testament to her time in Sellwood.

~ * ~

The silent apartment mocked Nash after the door shut behind Mia. With shaking hands, he pulled out the ring he'd retrieved from his safe deposit box the day before.

His mothers' wedding ring was perfect for Mia's small fingers. He'd been planning his proposal all week and wanted it to be perfect. Candlelight, soft music playing. The traditional one-knee stance, saying the right words to convince her he wanted all of her, no matter where they lived. Now what? Just let her go back to her old life without telling her how he felt?

Papa said anything worth having was worth fighting for.

~ * ~

On the drive back to the Rocking C, Mia had hours to think about her time in the city. As the miles flew by, she felt like a big piece of herself was being ripped from her chest. She'd left so much behind. Grams. Seth. And most importantly...Nash.

The last few miles of her trip she caught glimpses of a blue Explorer in her rearview mirror, raising her hopes, then dashing them again. Nash wouldn't follow her. She'd ruined the possibility of them by not thinking about him when it counted, then running like a scared little girl.

Finally the ranch came into view. Bright white sheep dotted the front pastures. She'd missed the annual sheering. The question was, did she care? Not really. The ranch wasn't her future, it was only a stepping stone.

As she parked, Gina ran out to the bunkhouse where Mia had her own room. Focused on her friend, she ignored the vehicle that pulled in behind her. It was probably one of her fellow ranch hands.

Her ginger-haired friend enveloped her in a tight hug. "I'm so glad you're back. Dad is too. He didn't want to lose his best hand."

Mia doubted that, but it was nice to hear. Gina stepped back with a quizzical frown before she could say anything.

"Who'd you bring with you?"

She turned to see Nash getting out of his dust-covered truck. Her heart leaped as hope blossomed. "What are you doing here?"

"Following my heart."

Stunned, she stammered, "Bb-but what about your practice?"

He shrugged like he didn't just toss out his five-year plan. "I'll follow you wherever your dream takes us. If you want to live in the wilds of Idaho, we'll check out the nearest town, see if they need a chiropractor."

"Hey, Midget's back." Her fellow ranch hands gathered in a semi-circle around them. "Who's the guy?"

"Wait—Midget has a boyfriend?"

Mia cringed at the nickname the guys gave her the first day on the job and focused on Nash's face.

"Awww, man…is he stealing our best hand?"

"Shhh, something's going on," Gina said.

Then everybody faded away as Nash knelt at her

feet and held up an antique ring. "Mia Belden, I love all of you. Would you do me the honor of becoming my wife?"

She urged him to stand, searching his face for any shred of doubt and didn't find it. It was humbling to think that he would close his office and move to Idaho if that was what she wanted.

Remembering her fantasy at the farm earlier that day, she knew she was done running. All her life she'd wanted roots, a foundation to build the rest of her life on. Her heart screamed that she'd found it. Being independent didn't mean diddly if you were alone.

To get her dream, all she had to say was..."Yes."

Nash kissed her fiercely. She heard hoots and hollers in the background, but ignored them for the fireworks going off in her heart.

EPILOGUE

Mia stood in the second story bedroom window that overlooked the back yard. Fifty or so of their favorite people gathered around near the drink and snack tables, waiting for the main event. The farm looked beautiful. It had taken her and Nash six long months to get it cleaned up for the wedding, but it had been worth it.

Grams chatted with John, giggling like a young girl. Good lord, was her grandmother flirting? Staying at Martha's Elder House was the best choice for the next couple of months while she regained her strength.

Dad was running a little late, but called to say he'd be there soon. They'd talked several times over the past months. She didn't have the father she'd wanted during her growing up years, but she cherished every moment she could spend with him now.

Gina knocked on the door frame as she entered the bedroom. "Are you ready?"

"Almost. I just need help with my veil."

Her ginger-haired friend looked gorgeous in her fitted bridesmaids' dress. Mia was pleased to see the green matched Nash's eyes and was the right color for Gina. Since her father was due to arrive any moment, she turned to look out the window again.

Nash stood near the minister, handsome in his black

suit and tie. He caught her gaze and with a grin that stole her breath, promised to be by her side the rest of his life.

The End

Other Books by **Darla Luke**:

The Haunted House Of Thomas Creek

**The Girl Most Likely To: An Anthology
(The Girl Most Likely To...Become The CEO)**

Keep reading for a preview of Book Three
in Sellwood Novella Series...

**Sealed With A Kiss
By Susan Lute**

One

"You're not wearing the dress I bought you."

The up and coming political star with aspirations for the U. S. Senate, was irritated.

Agnes wasn't surprised. She glanced down at the black leggings, emerald-green flowing top inset with slashes of lace, and her favorite Converse tennis shoes before opening the door wide as an invitation to enter.

She grabbed her cell from the side table where she'd left it. *Five o'clock? Crap!*

Scrambling to find an excuse that wouldn't irritate him further, the only thing she could conjure up was the truth. "I'm sorry. Picked up this sweet gig today. Identifying spyware. Worms. Intruders. The whole nine yards. I lost track of time."

She backed toward her bedroom and the dress that so wasn't her style.

Her consulting business, Cooper Cyber Securities, was her life. Well, with the exception of Todd, the guy she'd been dating for two years. And she loved it. The challenge. Excitement of the chase. Sussing out code gone wrong. Locking out hackers.

When her apology had no affect—Todd's brows pulled into an intimidating canyon—Agnes stopped retreating. Hands plunked on hips, not needing anyone to tell her what she should wear, she took a stand. Though a good girlfriend, just this once, would probably make an exception. If she was interested in talking him out of his foul mood.

She wasn't given a chance.

"My god, Agnes! When are you going to grow up and start living in the real world?"

Real world? What was he talking about? She had a real-world job. Agnes swallowed her sudden anger before she said something she shouldn't. "I said I was sorry. It won't take long to get ready. Ten minutes. Fifteen tops."

Before she could spin around and perform this miracle—really she'd need at the very least thirty minutes—Todd' next words stopped her cold.

"This isn't going to work for me."

She forced in a breath that didn't border on panic, let her fists drop from her hips, and hoped like hell this wasn't going the direction it sounded. The fact that Todd, who had the dark, handsome looks of a GQ cover model, had been with her for two years...now that was the real miracle. "This? What isn't working for you?"

His scowl didn't ease, plunging Agnes' stomach into a quagmire of queasy. His well-manicured hand flapped between them. "You and me."

She straightened her shoulders; stretched to her full five foot, four plus a quarter inch when she could manage it. "Why? Because I forgot about a silly date? The job I got today is important—"

"I'm sure it is," he dismissed her objection, brushing at invisible lint on his black Hugo Boss jacket. She knew the brand because he'd been sure to mention it a time or two or ten. "But this isn't the first time I'm going to be late for an important fund raiser because you *forgot*, and I can see now, it won't be the last."

Agnes narrowed her eyes, "Maybe you need a new girlfriend." The words slipped out before she could stop them.

"Maybe I do," he spat, heading for the door.

"Wait!" Fuming, she dashed to her closet, grabbed the offensive puke-yellow, off-the-rack dress from the hanger, and marching back to the living room, flung it at Todd. "Take this ugly thing with you."

His eyes glinted in equal temper. Agnes swallowed the lump growing in her throat. God. She'd been with this jerk for two years. She loved him. Didn't she? Did she really want to break up over a stupid, ugly dress? Or...anything else?

Todd practically sprinted for the door. Yanking the thing open, he turned at the last minute, slinging at her, "I've only stayed this long because you turn heads when you manage to dress appropriately for the occasion. I kept thinking you'd improve, but look at you. The joke was on me, wasn't it? And just so you know...not only are you the worst girlfriend I've ever had, you're a lousy kisser, too!"

Over his shoulder, Agnes saw Miles, fist raised to knock, the expression on his face as shocked as she felt. Fighting the moisture gathering in her eyes, she groaned in humiliation.

Todd didn't stay to see the devastation his words caused and Miles Preston had surely taken in enough. Swiping at the tears threatening to spill, She retreated to the kitchen before burying her face in her hands.

The last she heard from Todd was his snarled, "Out of my way," before the door closed with a sharp snap. Maybe Miles had done her a favor and escaped with the rat.

No such luck.

Strong arms wrapped around her shoulder and turned her gently toward a solid chest.

Argh! "You heard that," she wailed.

"Yes, I did," he said, his voice serious as a hundred dollar bill.

At least it wasn't pity she heard. Part of her was grateful. The rest silently screamed *No!*

Her relationship with Todd hadn't been perfect, but at least while they were together she wasn't that girl in her high school senior class, who'd been called four eyes all through grade school—still too skinny, and geeky, and in love with role playing games to get a date. When she finally had, she almost hadn't recovered from the resulting humiliation.

"Can you believe that guy?" she said into the solid man chest belonging to her best friend.

Miles pulled her hands from her face, lifting her chin so her swimming gaze met his. "He's a troglodyte."

"You're right. He *is* a troglodyte." She tilted back, pulled the stylish blue glasses from where they rested on top of her head and perched them on the bridge of her nose. As a defense barrier they worked pretty damn good. "Am I a bad kisser, Miles?"

A spark flashed in his green eyes for a second, then just as quickly disappeared. Her breath hitched before returning to normal. That wasn't supposed to happen. Not with Miles.

"Wouldn't know, would I? Best friend here. And the best-friend's handbook says absolutely no kissing."

Oh my god! He doesn't remember!

She'd met Miles at a party shortly after moving to Sellwood, and because they had gaming in common ended up in a corner chatting a good share of the evening. His friends from the gaming community wandered in and out of the conversation. She'd had a little more to drink than her strict one alcoholic beverage at social gatherings. After that things got a little fuzzy.

Miles had insisted on driving her home. But

standing out in her mind the next morning—and still hard to forget—was a rather mind-scrambling kiss on the doorstep and a shrugged suggestion they meet up at a local coffee shop the next week. She'd attributed the sizzle of crazy anticipation that stayed with her to the rare thrill of having a good-looking guy see the girl beneath her high-end computer skills.

When Thursday rolled around, she'd already met Todd at that same coffee shop the previous day, which since she worked from home, had become her favorite hangout. He'd been aggressive in his pursuit, flattering her long battered ego. The rest, as the saying went, was history. Not even her beloved mom and sister would have predicted Agnes Marie Cooper, the girl who hadn't been asked on a real date until senior prom, would end up with two gorgeous guys interested in her—one to become her boyfriend, the other the best friend she would ever have.

Agnes groaned. She'd have to tell her mom and Kelly, Todd—the troglodyte—had dumped her. If she could just lean on Miles' strength a moment longer...maybe she'd find the courage.

"He said I don't live in the real world."

She felt Miles' snort clear to the soles of her feet. "Of course you live in the real world. Todd is an ass."

Agnes laughed, a soft crackle of sound she couldn't stop from ending in a watery hiccup. "How come I can't keep a boyfriend? What am I going to do, Miles?"

"You need a distraction." He edged her onto the nearest bar stool. "I actually came over to talk to you about partnering up on a new game I'm developing."

"For Pendragon Games?" Pendragon was the fast-growing start-up company he worked for as a front end developer.

"No, this one's mine. We've got *Jaguar Guardian* far enough along, it's time to get someone on board to manage cyber security. I want that someone to be you."

When are you going to grow up? rang in her ears. She was comfortable in the smaller world of her cyber business, and liked the anonymity of CCS being the face she presented to the world. There was only one exception, but no one, not even Miles, knew about that little foray out of her box. "I don't know."

"I'll pay your going rate." Which he should know, since they'd had long discussions about her fee schedule when she'd first set up her consulting business.

A comforting hand massaged her shoulder. How had she not noticed how warm... and amazing...Miles' hands were?

She chewed her lip. "Maybe I should get a grownup job."

"Owning a successful consulting company *is* a grownup job." The first hint of annoyance darkened his usually easy-going expression. Miles' hands dropped to his sides. "Don't let this breakup with that jerk change who you are."

Agnes sighed. "And who am I, Miles?"

Taking a step back, he took in her appearance, his earnest gaze brushing her from head to toe. Sitting up straighter, she finger combed her hair to make sure it wasn't sticking out at all angles.

"Well, you're Agnes Cooper, owner and chief bottle washer for Cooper Cyber Securities. Your favorite TV show is *Bones*. You drink Oolong tea in the morning. Like cats and dogs, but can't decide which one to get, so no pets yet. You love bicycling, and would travel more if you didn't take on so much work. Alone time is your favorite time of day. Dressing up means jeggings and your favorite *Star Wars* tee shirt, the one with Chewbacca on the front. And nobody has as many Converse shoes as you do."

So even Miles viewed her as the girl next door who

could clean up any program glitch a person might encounter. His description proved she didn't have the sexy-girl vibe guys went out of their way to date. Staring at her feet comfortably encased in mint green Converses, she softly agreed, "I have a lot of them, don't I."

"Yup." Lips quirking up at the edges, Miles crossed his arms over his chest. "You're smart, funny, a little on the snarky side when you're buried in a project, but I like that about you."

He headed for the door. She followed him. "You have to like me. You're my best friend."

"Sure. Who else would want seconds of your spaghetti on the rare occasion you decide to cook?"

"I prefer the deli." Cooking wasn't her favorite thing. "Miles?"

"What?" He stopped with his hand on the door knob. His annoyance no longer flashed, but had it faded enough not to come roaring back to life at the shocking idea pushing to escape?

"You date a lot, right?"

"I wouldn't say a lot."

"But the point is, you kiss the girls, so you've had some practice and are probably a good kisser, I'm guessing." If her sketchy memory was correct, he was a damn fine kisser.

His eyes narrowed.

Agnes kind of questioned her sanity too, but nonetheless blurted out, "I could be a better kisser. A best friend would help me practice, wouldn't he?"

It was amazing really, seeing Miles shove a wall up between them, shutting her out as if they hadn't known each other for the best part of two years. He'd always been so open and transparent; the guy she could ask anything of, share anything with. Now he was looking at her with a stranger's eyes.

Being caught in that stare was almost worse than

having Todd dump her. Agnes' stomach knotted.

He yanked the door open. "Think about working on my game. I really need you on this project."

And then he was gone, leaving nothing behind. Not even his usual warm and cheery smile.

ABOUT THE AUTHOR

Darla Luke grew up in the concrete jungle of California. Her mother was an avid reader, instilling a love of the written word that lasted a lifetime. As a pre-teen, Darla spent many hours reading everything she could get her hands on...The Hobbit, Lord of the Rings trilogy (waayy before they became best-selling movies), and she dreamed of becoming a sleuth like Nancy Drew, or a side-kick to one of the Hardy Boys.

In her teen years, she discovered romance novels. Georgette Heyer. Barbara Cartland. And of course, the Harlequin Readers Club.

Now, she's a wife & mother living on a century farm in the heart of the Willamette Valley, Oregon. When she's not out tending to her chickens (who thinks she's a mobile food machine), she's either crocheting or writing.

If someone would have told her she'd be an author when she grew up, she would have laughed herself silly. Now one of her favorite things to do is to write about strong women and the rocky journey to find love with a deserving man.

To find out about new releases for the Sellwood
Novellas, visit Darla's website at
http://www.darlaluke.com
Or
http://www.susanlute.com

Thank you for reading **All Of You!** I hope you enjoyed
it. If you did, please help other readers find this book by
posting a review at any or all of your favorite review
sites.

This book is lendable: send it to a friend you think might
like it.